"You're ... You Were ...

She had lost control and aimed for the most vulnerable part of him, just as he had done earlier. In stark fear she watched the whitening of his face.

"You damned little witch!" he ground out, grabbing her arms to drag her against his lean, hard body. Josh's green eyes sparkled with diamond-hard hate, and a shivering began deep in her stomach and radiated throughout her entire body.

"What's the matter, Candra? Are you wishing I made love to *you* that day so long ago? Are you wondering what it would feel like to lie in my arms, have my hands on your soft flesh, caressing you, making love to you? Is that it?" He didn't allow her time to answer. His mouth came down in a kiss that took her breath away. She couldn't fight him, even after she realized the form his punishment was taking. . . .

RITA CLAY

has tried almost every job once. This former book-store manager also sold cosmetics, worked in a bank and ran her own modeling school before turning to writing. Now a successful romance author, she looks forward to describing the diversity and joys of love in many books to come.

Dear Reader:

SILHOUETTE DESIRE is an exciting new line of contemporary romances from Silhouette Books. During the past year, many Silhouette readers have written in telling us what other types of stories they'd like to read from Silhouette, and we've kept these comments and suggestions in mind in developing SILHOUETTE DESIRE.

DESIREs feature all of the elements you like to see in a romance, plus a more sensual, provocative story. So if you want to experience all the excitement, passion and joy of falling in love, then SILHOUETTE DESIRE is for you.

I hope you enjoy this book and all the wonderful stories to come from SILHOUETTE DESIRE. I'd appreciate any thoughts you'd like to share with us on new SILHOUETTE DESIRE, and I invite you to write to us at the address below:

Karen Solem
Editor-in-Chief
Silhouette Books
P.O. Box 769
New York, N.Y. 10019

Published by Silhouette Books, New York
America's Publisher of Contemporary Romance

RITA CLAY
Yesterday's Dreams

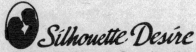

Silhouette Desire

Published by Silhouette Books New York

America's Publisher of Contemporary Romance

Other Silhouette Books by Rita Clay

Wanderer's Dream
Wise Folly
Sweet Eternity

 SILHOUETTE BOOKS, a Simon & Schuster Division of
GULF & WESTERN CORPORATION
1230 Avenue of the Americas, New York, N.Y. 10020

ISBN: 0-671-43608-2

First Silhouette Books printing December, 1982

10 9 8 7 6 5 4 3 2 1

America's Publisher of Contemporary Romance

Printed in the U.S.A.

To My Five Children,
Rebecca, Mark, Rita Lou,
Marissa and Clay

Yesterday's Dreams

1

Candra Bishop stood at the opened doors of her father's study and stared past the high brick patio, the rolling lawns and the slow moving Willamette River to the peak of the dormant volcano Mount Hood. To many it was the symbol of a journey's end. Settlers forging westward long ago had stared at that same peak in awe and wonder. They had made a treacherous journey to reach a piece of paradise. Tall mountains, rolling plains, wide rivers filled to the brim with fish and the deep blue Pacific Ocean not far away made Portland, Oregon, a land of opportunity for everyone. Everyone except Candra. But now her chance had come. She had an opportunity to prove that she too could search for that elusive mirage called happiness, or its other name— freedom.

"... And with the sale of the house and the money from the auction of your father's business yesterday, all debts should be paid off," Uncle Ralph, a family friend and her father's lawyer announced. "But I'm afraid that leaves little Roddy with a trust fund that can't be touched until his twenty-first birthday and you, my dear, with nothing but a burden."

"I have Roddy, Uncle Ralph. He'll never be a burden to me." Candra continued to stare at the snowcapped peak. The breeze ruffled her dark brown hair and molded the pale blue shirtwaist dress against her slim body. She was beautiful, there was no doubt about it, Uncle Ralph thought; if she hadn't been so beautiful and so willful, would Alicia have treated her any better? He doubted it. Roddy showed little promise of growing as tall and handsome as she was. Perhaps that was why he had been so neglected until Candra had returned from school and had taken over as "little mother." Candra had taken Roddy to her heart as if he was her own child.

"Are you going to take your uncle up on his offer?" He coughed nervously. "Do you think you'll live with him?"

Candra glanced over her shoulder at the slim balding man, not surprised that he should know of her uncle's offer which had arrived by letter. He had offered a home of sorts to both her and Roddy as long as she was willing to work at the inn he owned and operated. It wasn't a home that was opened to her with love, only obligation. But at least it was offered. She might find working for a living a little hard after years of living without financial worries, but it was her work that would feed and clothe them. That thought held out a beautiful promise of independence that was more than welcome.

"I think so, unless you can recommend something else?" She smiled teasingly at him, knowing that it hurt him to see her leave this house almost as much as it hurt her.

"I thought you and Jamie Dieterman . . ." He trailed off as the smile left Candra's face. He should have known that Jamie's mother wouldn't want that relationship to continue now that Candra lacked the one commodity the Dietermans needed most— money. Jamie and Candra were well matched for looks and breeding, not to mention charm, but the Dieterman family needed money so they would be able to continue the lifestyle that meant so much to them.

Candra turned back to stare at Mount Hood. The memories the scene should have stirred were dormant. Although her eyes were locked on the massive mountain, the fact didn't register at all.

"It's one thing to marry Henry Bishop's darling daughter, but quite another to marry a penniless orphan. It sounds like something from a Victorian novel, doesn't it? Yet the auctioneer tells me that thousands of businesses a year go into bankruptcy and onto the auction block. This was just another one of many to him."

"I wish Dieterman had a little more spunk, though. Why with your beauty . . ." he began, only to be interrupted.

"And a young brother to care for, not to mention an inn to run, I should be kept very busy. Too busy for marriage for quite some time." She turned, finally taking pity on the older man. It wasn't his fault that he thought her world had crashed, even though she knew better. She was looking forward to, in fact was eager to begin, her role in her new life. "Uncle Ralph, I do believe you're a romantic!"

"And so should you be, young lady!" he sputtered, blushing. "Everyone needs to be a romantic at some time in life. It's as necessary to the soul as water to the rose."

Candra gave a mock salute, showing for a brief moment the old Candra, the one from before her father's remarriage. "Yes, sir. I'll remember that, sir."

The lawyer fidgeted with the papers strewn across the desk, obviously not finished with the discussion, yet not knowing how to go on. He peered at her over his spectacles, then quickly looked back at his papers when he realized she was watching him, a question in her deep blue eyes.

"What is it?" she asked softly, taking a step into the center of the room. When he once again looked up the words he was about to say clogged in his throat. She was a lovely vision. Her hair was a brown so dark that it was highlighted with black, complementing her striking blue eyes and clear creamy complexion. Her slim figure was well rounded, but what really made her unique was her aloof, carefully guarded expression. Her almost queenly reserve arrested most people's attention. Very rarely did she let down her guard to show the true Candra. Only when she was with her little brother and a few close friends was she buoyant and vivacious enough to show a glimpse of her more personal self.

"Uncle Ralph?"

"Well, one man, a Mr. Laurence, bought the three largest pieces of equipment and paid top dollar for them. I don't need to tell you how important that sale was. Without it we would still be several thousand in the hole as far as your father's debts. His only request was that you were to deliver the contracts within forty-eight hours."

Candra stiffened, her hands involuntarily clenching together. "Mr. Laurence? What's his first name?"

"I can't remember exactly." The lawyer searched through the papers scattered on the top of the desk, finally finding the right one. "Yes, here it is. A Mr. Scott Laurence. Rather an odd duck. He gave us the highest bid over the phone, sight unseen, and asked to have the equipment sent directly to one of the Indian reservations. I believe he's a recluse, lives down on the Rogue River between Agness and Gold Beach. Since it's on your way to San Francisco I took the liberty of agreeing for you." He glanced up, noticing for the first time how pale she had become. "Is it all right? I can cancel for you and take them myself."

"No, it's fine. I thought for a moment it might be someone I knew." Candra walked back toward the French doors, once again caught in thoughts of the past. "I thought it was someone I knew," she repeated slowly to herself, the words echoing in the silent room.

"You know, Candra, you don't have to live with your uncle. After all, you hardly know him. He and your father never did see eye to eye about anything, especially business. You and Roddy are welcome to live with Dora and me. We would always be happy to have you. I've known you such a long time, and although there was nothing I could do to help you with Alicia, I *can* help you now." He swallowed hard, loath to bring up the woman's name for fear of stirring up bad memories. Some things were best forgotten.

"But now you're grown up and I had hoped she couldn't hurt you anymore. I never guessed she'd run through all that money!" He shook his head once again, this time taking off his glasses to wipe them with a crisp white handkerchief. His myopic gaze centered on the blurred form walking toward him to give a soft hug to his rounded shoulders.

"I know and I thank you for the offer." She spoke slowly, choosing her words carefully so he wouldn't be offended in any way. He was the only person she could talk to and she wanted him to understand. No one else mattered. "I think the years in boarding school did me some good after all, Uncle Ralph. I learned to stand up for myself. I wasn't judged for my father's money as much as for my own merits and ability." She smiled impishly. "And now I find that I'll have to live on that ability and I'm eager to find where my talents lie. I know I didn't learn a skill, but I've still got my wits."

"And Roddy?" he asked gently.

"And Roddy belongs with me. He's been mine for

the past six years. I see no reason to change that now."

"But he's your half-brother, not your son!"

"Does it matter? I took his mother's place years ago. He stays with me," she stated matter-of-factly, closing the discussion by visibly withdrawing.

The older man nodded, knowing it was useless to question her decisions any further. "And you don't think Roddy will resent not living here, where he's lived all his life?"

"I think Roddy already knows that all this home stands for is a larger roof and richer food than others have. That's not exactly important for a seven-year-old. Other things mean more to him. We both found that out the hard way."

"Alicia must have hurt you very deeply, Candra." He sighed.

"On the contrary. Alicia taught me just what I would be like if I continued to live her kind of life. I was lucky, and I know it. When I was thirteen and she married Daddy I was a spoiled brat. I hurt people terribly and without real reason." The burning sensation in her eyes told her that tears weren't far away. Memories came back to flood her with emotions she had thought frozen. Would she ever forget the tall thin young man laughing in the sun, a guitar strapped across his chest as he played for a precocious thirteen-year-old pest? She had repaid him so well. She had stamped *final* on a friendship that had meant more to her than living and breathing. "I behaved so badly," she murmured, once more caught in another time.

The lawyer shuffled the last of the papers into his beaten up briefcase, snapping it shut with finality. He had to be home for dinner or Dora would worry. He still had to take the bridge across the river into Washington and it would be rush hour soon.

"Are you sure you can deliver these contracts on your way?"

"Mr. Laurence will get his contracts within the forty-eight hours he stipulated."

"Good. And if you need me I'll be as close as the phone, my dear. Independence is a fine thing, but it isn't all it's cracked up to be." With that he kissed her on the cheek and left the house. Candra could hear the door shut and, for the first time since the funeral, she was totally alone. The last of the servants had been in the process of leaving even as Uncle Ralph had arrived. Roddy was at a friend's house, saying good-bye. Her father and stepmother were gone and would never return. Even the life she had known up to now was gone, leaving her strangely adrift in a sea of anchored ships. For the first time since the funeral she felt the tears trickle down her cheeks and she shook her head in silent denial. There wasn't time to let go of her emotions. There wasn't time for anything except saying good-bye to Gabriel Manor before embarking on her new life.

She walked through the French doors and out to the patio. The weather was uncommonly warm and the sunshine was a blessing in early March. The well-kept lawn stretched down to the river. The bushes would be ready to be pruned soon, but the new owners would have to see to that. Everything that would happen to the house and garden in spring would be up to the new owners.

Candra looked toward the east, through the trees, to the rooftop of the neighboring house. Bettina Wallace used to live there before the scandal. After the trouble Candra had created, the Wallaces had moved and new people had bought their home, just as new people would now own this one. Would they care for it as her family had? Would they realize the love and planning that had gone into every brick?

Candra's eyes swept westward, through another stand of trees to the barn. They used to own horses for riding, but four years ago Alicia had finally convinced her father to sell them and turn the barn into a gigantic playroom. Alicia had hated horses and hated even more the time Henry spent riding them. She had always needed his undivided attention and admiration and most of the time she had received it. Once the horses were gone she had it all. Before that though, there had been a constant flurry of activity surrounding the barn: grooms walked the horses, hay pitched in stalls, grains mixed in buckets, the smell of leather and animal blending together to form an atmosphere of sane and safe comfort. It had been a wonderful world then. Candra was constantly running in and out, talking to her heart's content, spilling her hopes and dreams in Josh's lap like bright-colored marbles and he took those dreams and molded her childish enthusiasms to make them sound more like reality. He had been her brother, friend and mentor. Until that day . . .

A breeze whipped her skirt and sent a chill to raise

goose bumps on her arms. She walked down the steps to the ground, taking the small paved path around the side of the house to the front. The large two-story edifice was filled with more than antiques. It was filled with memories. The first memories were lovely, of a time when her mother and father were both alive, dreaming of a future for them and their daughter. Then came the unhappy times, after her mother died delivering a stillborn son. Everything had changed then. Her father had withdrawn from Candra as if she brought thoughts to the forefront that should have been forgotten. He completely immersed himself in work at the furniture factory, working day and night. Candra was raised by the cook, the gardener, the maid, then, finally, Josh. But by the time Josh entered her world Candra was a spoiled demanding child, asking loudly and receiving whatever she asked for to quiet her. She got everything, except her father's love.

A large Lincoln wound up the drive to stop near Candra. The back door opened and Roddy came bounding out, dragging his best friend Tim along behind him. Roddy's brown eyes implored her to give the correct answer even before he asked the question. "Tim's mom says I can come back to spend the last week before school starts with them. Can I, Candra?" The words tumbled out and over themselves as he hopped from one foot to the other, holding tight to Candra's hand as if that would ensure the right response. Everyone wanted an answer from her, but at least this was one she was willing and able to give.

"That's very nice of Tim's mother and I'm sure it can be arranged, Roddy," she promised, hoping other promises would be kept as well. Promises of a roof over their heads, food in their stomachs, clothing . . .

She and Roddy watched Tim run back to the car. Tim's mother, Evelyn, and Candra had already said their good-byes. Evelyn had been a good friend to her, one of the few people she would miss. She waved as Evelyn drove past her and continued toward the large iron gates that marked the entrance of the property, and a feeling of sadness almost overwhelmed her. Another phase of life had passed and she had to change, whether she wanted to or not.

Candra turned, placing her hand on Roddy's shoulder, and made her way up the stone steps of Gabriel Manor. It was time to get Roddy into his bath and put dinner on the table. They had to leave early in the morning if she was to deliver those papers. Suddenly she was cold again and a chill swept through her body to travel down her spine. She ignored it. This was no time to get cold feet!

2

The Oregon weather was acting like a woman again, showing its fickle ways. Only yesterday it had been brisk but beautiful and this morning it was cold, gray and cloudy. A perfect day to leave Gabriel Manor, Candra mused as she sipped on hot coffee and watched the Willamette churning against its banks.

It was time to wake Roddy and get him dressed and fed. Candra refilled her cup and walked out of the kitchen and down the long paneled hallway toward the curving teakwood staircase. Everything had been sorted, cleaned and packed. All that was left was to fill the car with their belongings and leave.

She reached the top of the stairs and turned left, following the long runner toward Roddy's room, only one room before hers.

"Rise and shine, sleepyhead! Time to get dressed and eat!" She pulled the covers off the reluctant child, who was still burrowing into the pillow.

"Ummmm, just five more minutes, please, Candra?" he mumbled groggily.

"I already gave you five minutes before I came in here. So it's now or never."

"You're mean!" he moaned and Candra winced even though she knew he hadn't meant it. Someone else had called her that once. She turned her thoughts in another direction.

"I may be mean, but that's the way it is," she retorted sharply. "Now, come on. We still have to load the car."

She left the room when Roddy jumped out of bed, a contrite expression on his face as he ran toward the bathroom. She sighed with exasperation. Now that he was up she knew it would only be a matter of minutes before he was dressed and asking for breakfast.

Candra barely had breakfast ready by the time Roddy bounded down the stairs. Her little brother was looking upon the journey to their uncle's home as an adventure, a belief which she had reinforced to some degree. All children were resilient at seven years old. He would be able to make the changes necessary for their new way of life; for her it would be more difficult. But she would do it, she had to, if only for Roddy's sake. There wasn't much she wouldn't do for him.

Within the hour they had eaten and cleaned up the last of the dishes, leaving the kitchen spotless.

They loaded the car to the brim with luggage and the trunk with boxes of "'portant things" that Roddy didn't think he could do without. A few of his favorite books, some games, a small photo album, a wooden box filled with rocks and pieces of wood were all necessary items in his mind. By the time everything was done it was already one o'clock. Oh, well, Candra thought, they could get lunch along the way.

She stood next to the car, a shining midnight blue Cadillac Seville, that would take them away and glanced back at the house. The car had been her twenty-second birthday gift from her father and one of the few things that was all hers. She smiled; at least she shouldn't have any transportation problems for awhile!

"Say good-bye, Roddy." She glanced down at the small dark-haired boy who stood so silently beside her as he contemplated the house.

"It's just a house, Candi. I don't need the house as long as you're here," the child said with more insight than most adults. He squeezed Candra's hand as if to give comfort before scrambling into the car.

"California, here we come!" he cried, his fist in the air as if leading a charging army.

"We're not going straight to California, nut."

"But we'll get there," he reasoned. "Then I can say I've been to three states. Washington, Oregon, where I was born, and California, where I'll go to school."

Candra laughed. "You're right, punkin. And more

knowledgeable than I realized. I'll have to be careful or you'll be smarter than I am in no time!''

They left the drive giggling. It felt good that they could leave what had been their home and still find something to laugh about. Perhaps it was an omen of things to come.

From the moment they were on Highway Five the weather took on an increasingly gloomy aspect; the sky turned darker and heavier by the mile. The storm was going to be a big one. How big, Candra couldn't begin to guess. She only hoped she would be able to reach Mr. Laurence's home quickly. She glanced at her mileage indicator. She had gone almost one hundred miles; the turnoff wouldn't be too much further ahead. Suddenly the sky opened up and the heavy rain that poured down obscured the road ahead almost completely.

"Hand me the envelope in my purse, Roddy, will you?'' she asked after a little while, keeping her eye on the road. The downpour was now changing into a light sleet. Rainclouds blanketed the sky as far as the eye could see.

"Is it much farther?'' her half-brother asked, stifling a yawn brought on by inactivity. He passed the large white envelope to his sister and she slowed down even more so she could read the directions.

The Canyonville exits came up and Candra pulled into the access road, once again reading the instructions carefully. She turned onto another small highway and followed the road to Agness. The sleet was turning to hail, then back to sleet again, making driving a slow, tedious process.

They passed Agness and continued to follow the Rogue River, heading toward the Pacific coast. Somewhere along here was supposed to be a cutoff to the right, with a small sign pointing the way to Dreamer's Cove. It came up sooner than she expected and she had to brake hard, almost slipping into a tailspin. But she straightened the wheel and gave a sigh of relief. So much for driving on sleet!

The luxury car gave hardly any indication of the dips and chuck holes in the rough road, but the wipers were barely keeping up with the slushy rain that poured down. Candra kept a white-knuckled hold on the steering wheel as she slowly followed the erratic track, having a hard time distinguishing the road from the ditch.

She was supposed to go approximately two miles before she would reach the house. In this weather she hoped she would see her destination before she drove into it! Just as Candra saw the dim lights of a house, the wheel pulled sharply to the left, almost depositing the car in the ditch.

She sat back, expelling a deep breath in hopes of controlling her frustration. "Well, that just about does it! I think we've got a flat. This old gentleman had better be nice enough to put up with us for the night. I don't think I could drive anymore in this weather, let alone fix a flat!" She put her foot back on the gas and slowly, very slowly, continued toward the house. What would have taken two minutes in dry weather took them more than ten. She stopped in the front of a large barn that had been converted into a huge home. A large veranda circled the front and sides and the lights shining through the darkness made it look like a cheery haven. Candra took no time at all in bundling Roddy under her arm and carrying him out of the car and through the sleet toward the dry, welcoming porch.

A short, stocky older man wearing a yellow slicker and hat that covered everything but his weathered skin and twinkling brown eyes opened the wide door, smiling as he came toward her. Suddenly she was aware of her hair hanging in strings down her back. Glancing at Roddy, Candra realized he had gotten soaked too. They both needed a change of clothing before they caught pneumonia.

"Good evening, ma'am. I think you two had better get out of those wet clothes, so if you'll give me your keys I'll get the luggage out of your car so you and the little one can change." His dark eyes and gentle smile relaxed Candra at once. She was too emotionally drained to ask questions at this moment. Obviously she was expected and he knew exactly who she was and why she was here. In time she would learn his name. He took the keys from her outstretched hand and turned, bowing his head against the rain as he shouted above the noise of the storm. "Go inside. The living room has a fire and there's some wine on the coffee table. I'll be right back."

It didn't take any more urging on his part to propel Candra inside the door. Both she and Roddy were chilled, not only by the rain but also by the temperature, which had been steadily dropping since they had left Portland. She wondered if the storm had hit at home or had begun down here. Not home, she corrected herself, Gabriel Manor. Someone else's home now.

Roddy's teeth were chattering and Candra emptied herself of all thoughts except taking care of him. She ushered him across the large room and over to the fire, peeling off his now damp sweater and rubbing his hands in hers to get his circulation back. Roddy wasn't the healthiest of children; childhood illnesses and colds always hit him more violently than they did most others, and wet clothing wasn't going to help matters. She wasn't going to be able to leave tonight under any conditions or Roddy's health would be in jeopardy. She only hoped her host would understand and could accommodate her and Roddy. He could sleep on the couch and she could use the floor, if necessary.

Her thoughts turned to her mysterious host. Was the older man in the slicker Mr. Laurence? Somehow she doubted it. He didn't look like a reclusive millionaire tycoon who bought and sold heavy duty equipment designed to turn lumber into beautiful tables and chairs and donated it to an Indian reservation.

A full decanter of wine sat on the coffee table and after pouring herself a glass and giving Roddy a sip, she looked around the room.

It was definitely a barn that had been converted, and converted very nicely. Apparently the owner hadn't allowed expense to get in his way. The living room had a wall of cedar and a huge rock fireplace separating it from whatever was in back of it. Behind her, where the tack room would have been, was a complete and extremely modern kitchen done in natural woods. Cheery yellow walls complemented the bright copper-colored appliances and brass utensils hanging jauntily just below the cabinets.

The floor was of highly polished cedar, as were the stairs that led up to a loft of some sort. Below the stairs was a raised dais holding a very contemporary and expensive chrome and glass dining room suite. Two large chairs flanked the fireplace, with equally large hassocks standing in front of them, while a giant paprika-colored couch covered in rich corduroy stood in front of the blazing fire. The door on the far right side of the fireplace must lead to another room, she surmised before turning her attention back to Roddy. He was curled up on the couch, watching the fire, his eyes half-closed. He sniffled, rubbing his nose on his shirtsleeve before Candra could pull a handkerchief out of her purse.

"The man is bringing your clothing, darling. In just a minute I'll have you dry and warm," she crooned, pushing his damp curling ringlets away from his small, heart-shaped face. Poor darling. His entire world had been turned topsy-turvy and he was still being so good.

"I'm fine, Candra, I'm just hungry, that's all," he murmured, holding tight to her hand.

"Well, that's going to be taken care of too, darlin'," she began, only to be interrupted when the door banged open and the man in the yellow slicker entered. He quickly pushed the suitcases with his foot while carrying two large boxes in his hands.

"Please," Candra exclaimed, "you didn't need to bring everything in. I only wanted a change of clothing for my brother!" But he continued to push the suitcases in with his foot, then turned and, dropping the boxes, closed the door. The cold draft that had followed him in immediately disappeared.

The nameless man grinned. "It seemed better that I bring them all, yes?" For the first time Candra noticed an accent in his speech. It sounded Spanish, but she wasn't sure. He held out his work-roughened hand. "I'm Pepe O'Con, Mr. Laurence's mechanic, carpenter, sometime-cook and everything else. Mr. Laurence will be here in awhile; he's finishing up on some work." He smiled again. "May I show you to your room?" he asked politely.

He was very kind and easygoing, but Candra got the feeling that everything had been prearranged. It was the way he said "your room," as if he already knew that she'd be staying. She shrugged, turned to take Roddy's hand and then followed Pepe, ignoring the chill premonition that settled over her. A cold that had nothing to do with the weather seemed to seep into her senses, alerting her to a danger she couldn't see, hear or smell. Once again she tried to shrug it off, but her mind was so tired that she could no longer control her emotions with her usual tight rein.

They walked up the staircase and along the landing which overlooked the living area. The glossy beams that had seemed so high when she was by the fire now seemed close enough to touch, their rich patina glowing in the dim lighting.

Candra almost bumped into Pepe as he stopped to open a door and stepped back to allow her entrance. Twin beds with bright orange spreads stood along the right wall, a small night table separating them. The left wall held a closet, slightly opened, and another door.

"This is the bath, ma'am," Pepe explained. "And the next room is yours. The bathroom connects them. I'll bring up the luggage while you give the little one a warm bath to take away the chill." His smile deepened. "I hope the beds will be comfortable for you. I noticed you had the boy's pillow in the car; I'll get it for him. He'll sleep better with it."

"I didn't mean for us to be such trouble for you, Pepe. I was only going to drop off the papers Mr. Laurence needed, not spend the night, but with this weather and the flat tire . . ."

"Mr. Laurence understands."

Before she could respond he was gone, the door quietly shut behind him. She had so many questions to ask, but she was too tired to form the words. Suddenly everything caught up with her and she was lonely, scared and desperately tired. She had just reached the first destination in her new life and already she was exhausted! It might have been only late afternoon, but her body ached as if it was midnight. She had been fighting not only storms, but painful memories and an unknown future as well. Well, the time for retrospection was over; the present called for action.

Candra began helping Roddy out of his wet clothes, then filled the tub with hot water. His bath wouldn't take long and then she would be able to get him some dinner, then into bed. She heard Pepe bring the rest of the luggage up to the second room as she handed a washcloth to Roddy. "Here, darling, wash yourself while I get some clean pajamas for you." She smiled at the sleepy boy; Roddy had no more energy to answer than she did to open suitcases, but it had to be done.

She opened the connecting door and stepped into what would be her room for the night, her eyes lighting up in pleasure and delight. The room was basically the same as Roddy's but it was done in biscuit and white and had a double bed. A large fluffy rug was at the side of the bed that was itself covered with a yellow and white spread. The curtains were of the same pattern and on the wall was a painting of a river flowing past a green lawn with yellow daisies growing along the bank. Somehow it reminded her of Gabriel Manor and tears stung her eyes. Stop it! she told herself sharply as she grabbed the suitcase and flung it on the bed. For years she hadn't liked what the house represented, so why was she homesick now? Once they were settled in their uncle's inn and had a routine, she would feel secure again.

As soon as Roddy was dressed in warm pajamas and robe and Candra had refreshed herself with a wash and touched up her makeup, they made their way down the stairs. She was sure that Mr. Laurence wouldn't care that Roddy wasn't dressed for dinner.

It had been too trying a day to ask for more than cleanliness.

Pepe was in the kitchen, busily taking a delicious smelling casserole of chicken and asparagus, if Candra's nose was correct, out of the oven. He turned, smiling, as he motioned to the large dining room table tucked beneath the stairs.

"Please sit. Mr. Laurence will be right with you. If you would like a glass of wine there's some on the sideboard." He slipped a loaf of French bread into the oven, set the timer and clicked the door shut with a snap. Roddy pulled himself up on a barstool by the counter and began riddling him with questions. Was this really a barn? Yes. Did it have animals? Yes, but now they lived in a new barn. Why did he want to live in a barn?

Candra poured herself a glass of wine, then slowly walked over to the bookcase built into a side wall and perused the titles. She found everything from the latest spy bestsellers to Dickens, and all the books had the look of being thoroughly read. She glanced back at her purse which she had left on one of the side tables when she came down. The documents were safely tucked away inside and she could hand them to Mr. Laurence as soon as he joined her, along with her apology for intruding on his hospitality.

Which brought up the next question for her dulled mind to ponder: Where was Mr. Laurence?

She turned toward the kitchen. "Pepe, when do you expect Mr. Laurence?"

The dark man looked up from answering a question for Roddy, his gaze slipping past her to the doorway on the far right, his face wreathed in a smile.

"Mr. Laurence is expected now," a deep, velvety rough voice said from the doorway behind her and Candra froze to the stillness of a statue. No, it couldn't be! The years suddenly melted away, leaving her once again as young, confused and vulnerable as she had been nine years ago, at thirteen. Her tired brain floundered like a lost ship on a rocky coast. Even now, as it had so long ago, an impotent jealousy mixed with frustrated anger rose in her throat to overwhelm her. She turned slowly to face her adversary.

"Hello, Candra. Welcome to Dreamer's Cove." Joshua Laurence stood leaning against the doorway, arms crossed against his broad chest. The full sensuous lips that spoke of passion were pressed together to make a tight, cynical line. His green eyes flashed with the hardness of emeralds and took her breath away. His dark hair was wet, as if he had just come from the shower, and he brushed it negligently away from his forehead with a strong bronzed hand, almost as if he wanted to do the same with her. He assessed her as she stared, her blue eyes showing the depths of her whirling emotions while he coldly raked her body as if he had stripped every bit of her clothing from her . . . and found her wanting.

He was the same as he had been all those years ago, only now the lines of age had formed a veneer of sophisticated cynicism around his eyes and mouth. The warmth that used to be such a part of him had turned to cold hard stone. It was frightening and her heart strayed to her throat to almost choke her. "Josh," she whispered, dropping her glass from frozen fingers to shatter in a thousand pieces against the polished floor. It was not only the wine glass that was broken; it was the carefully constructed wall of composure Candra had built over the years since their last meeting.

She continued to stare at him, unaware of the unnatural hush that cloaked the room. Her mind darted in so many directions that her thoughts were as fragmented as the broken glass. Had he arranged this meeting on purpose? Was he trying to punish her for what she had done all those years ago? Did he still hate her so much? The answers screamed in her mind. The cold and calculating look in his eyes gave her the answer she didn't want to know—yes.

But how far would his vendetta go?

3

~~~~~~~~~~~~~~

Why, Josh?" she finally asked, her voice hoarse with emotion. "Why would you hate someone so much after all these years that you'd go out of your way for vengeance?" Her voice sounded far away to her, as if someone else was uttering her thoughts. All her attention was so riveted on the imposing man in front of her that she was oblivious to Pepe mopping up the broken glass and the spill of deep red wine at her feet. Her eyes were locked with Josh's in a silent battle, only she wasn't sure what she was fighting for. Her breathing was shallow and the clenched hands at her sides were damp with tension. "Is this your perverted idea of a joke?"

Josh pulled away from the doorjamb, walking toward her slowly, as if stalking a small, cornered rabbit. The corners of his mouth rose in a chilly semblance of a smile. "Did you bring the papers, Candra? As I recall, you're supposed to be playing messenger boy."

He held out his hand expectantly and Candra bent to retrieve her purse from the side table, noticing for the first time that Pepe was cleaning up the mess she had made.

"Thank you, Pepe. I'm sorry I was so clumsy," she said quietly as he swept the last bit of glass into the dustpan. He smiled and nodded before returning to the kitchen.

"My, my, aren't we polite," Josh sneered. "Who are you trying to impress, I wonder? Pepe or myself?"

"Certainly not you." Candra slapped the papers into his outstretched hand and snapped her purse shut. She threw it on the couch as if it were a gauntlet, her eyes blazing with anger.

"That's a change. If I remember correctly you were always trying to impress someone—usually me—and when that didn't work your policy was vengeance, as only a girl-shrike could exact."

"I was thirteen, an unstable age at the best of times, and I thought I needed your security in those days." She choked on a bubble of hysterical laughter. They could have been talking about something that had happened yesterday instead of nine years ago. "I thought you could do no wrong. You were my personal saint and savior, until you finally showed me your feet of clay." She gave a slight, mocking curtsey. "I should thank you for that lesson. It taught me never to trust a man." He voice shook with pent-up frustration and anger. She knew she shouldn't be so open in her hatred, but she couldn't seem to control herself.

"Don't tell me you've grown up mentally as well as physically?" His eyes mocked the innocent question in his voice, taking in her slim figure from her toes to her dark hair, flickering with iridescent highlights in the firelight. "Could it be that, just like the rest of us mortals, Princess Candra had lessons to learn?" His voice was much harsher than she remembered and she flinched as if he had slapped her.

Roddy, who had been watching quietly up to this point, scooted off the stool and ran to Candra's side, where he slipped his hand into hers. His large brown eyes stared up at her, worry and confusion evident on his small face. Roddy could take any change in life as long as Candra was there and he would protect her with childish valor from other people who might hurt her. Protecting Candra was protecting himself. She glanced down and saw the indecision in his small face and knew what thoughts lay behind his tight handclasp. They had had to stand united against others too often in the past for Roddy not to know that this was just one more time. She stooped to give the small boy a reassuring hug, hoping to calm him, even if she wasn't quite under control herself.

"It's all right, punkin," she murmured softly. "But it's time to get dressed up warm so we can drive to Uncle Ted's. We don't want to take advantage of Mr. Laurence's hospitality any more than we have to."

"Don't be ridiculous," said Josh firmly, but with

more softness, as if realizing the state of the child's unsettled emotions. "Between the flat tire on your car and the foggy conditions outside there's no possible way for you to leave here this evening."

"But I . . ." she began, trying to grasp at any straw that might grant her safety from the hateful intensity of Josh's feelings.

"Are you expecting Pepe to trek out in the biting cold and rain to fix your tire for you?" he asked derisively, his expression showing more than words just how little he thought of her and her selfish whims. "You never did seem to care about other people unless that caring corresponded with your own wishes."

Candra was too tired and too confused to argue. Besides, she could think of nothing that wouldn't bring another stinging retort from him. She brushed a hand across her brow.

"Is there a hotel in the area? I could call a cab."

"No. You'll have to compromise yourself and spend the night here, whether you like it or not." He turned in a single fluid movement, not waiting for her answer. "Pepe? Is dinner ready?" At the older man's nod Josh walked toward the dining room table. Candra hesitated in the center of the room, clutching Roddy's hand. Her confused mind whirled with alternatives, each discarded just as quickly as it came. She looked down at her little brother, realizing just how tired the child was, and decided that before she did anything she had to take care of his needs.

Reluctantly, she followed Josh to the table. As soon as they sat down Pepe brought the large casserole to the table, along with warm French bread and a crisp spinach salad. Josh poured white wine for himself and Candra, while Pepe brought a large glass of chocolate milk for Roddy, winning a big smile for his efforts.

Candra felt the heated antagonism hanging in the air like a heavy mist. Only Roddy's presence kept it from swallowing them up. He ate heartily, despite his drooping eyelids and occasional yawns.

Candra ate sparingly, knowing that the food was delicious, but too confused by Josh's presence to be able to enjoy anything. When they had finished the main course Pepe brought a gelatin mold of squiggly orange, lemon and lime, which totally enchanted Roddy. Candra forgot that Josh was there as she watched Roddy giggle with delight at the simple treat. Alicia would have died if she had been served such a plebeian dessert. Candra's heart once more went out to the child who was in reality her half-brother but felt more like her son. He was the only person she had ever known who took love and gave it back three-fold.

"It seems you've found at least one person who doesn't suffer from your sour disposition, Candra." Josh leaned back, watching Roddy eat. "Surprising that it should be a child. Or is it that he doesn't demand emotions from you that might have to be reciprocated in a grown-up manner?"

His words sickened her. She *had* behaved that way when she was a child—selfish, demanding, totally self-centered. But Alicia had taught her, as no one else could have, just where that type of behavior could lead and, though Josh might never believe it, she had changed. She ignored the flip-flop of her stomach and raised her chin with a determined tilt so he would think his words hadn't hurt.

Josh took another drink of his Chablis. "It's odd that Henry was so sharp when it came to business, yet as a father he allowed his own child to become a spoiled brat." He took another sip of wine before noticing Roddy's hurt expression and trembling bottom lip as the small boy stared at him. He ruffled the boy's fine dark hair and slowly smiled. Candra knew and remembered that smile. She also knew that it would never be directed at her again. There had been a time when she had considered that it belonged to her alone—but that time was past. Her own jealous behavior had seen to that.

"But he seems to have done a pretty good job with the half-pint, so maybe it was the material he had to work with. Poor Henry."

"His name is Mr. Bishop to you." All caution flew to the wind. "For someone who worked in our stables you have a very elevated opinion of yourself. Don't stretch old friendship too far, Mr. Laurence. You're still not half the man he was, even at his worst."

He sat back in his chair, one hand absently twirling the wine glass in front of him. His face held the look of a satisfied cat, as if getting her to give in to her anger had pleased him.

"Are you asking me to change my mind about the

deal to buy the machinery?" he questioned in a dangerously soft voice, one winged brow raised mockingly.

Her shoulders stiffened, then drooped in defeat as the light of battle left her eyes. "No." He had to know that there was no way the machinery could be sold at that high price twice.

"Then you had better be aware of your manners, Miss Bishop. For your own sake."

Roddy spoke up, his voice wavering. "Don't you talk to my sister that way! She's mine!" His bright eyes widened as he skirted Josh's chair and flung himself into Candra's lap, as if shielding her from the other man's contempt. His small chest heaved, as if he was trying to hold back the tears that threatened to spill.

Josh smiled in apology. It was his second smile since they had arrived and it completely changed his face from cold and distant to warm and inviting. "I'm sorry, little one. I didn't mean to hurt your feelings," he soothed. He went on when he saw the sleepy reluctance on Roddy's face. "Why don't you sit back down and enjoy your dessert? I promise I'll be good." He glanced toward the kitchen. "Pepe made it especially for you."

His diversionary tactics succeeded immediately, much to Candra's chagrin.

"Pepe made this just for me?" Roddy looked past Candra's shoulder toward the older man puttering in the kitchen, as he returned to his seat. Pepe grinned, nodding in silent assent.

Candra's heart swelled with love as she saw the delighted wonder in her brother's eyes. "What do you say, Roddy?" she prompted softly.

"Thank you, Mr. Pepe. It's very good." And he took another lopsided bite just to prove it. "Can we make some of this when we get to our uncle's house, Candra?"

"Let's wait and see, punkin," Candra answered, hoping he'd eat quickly so they could disappear upstairs as soon as possible. Her nerves were already stretched to the breaking point. Any more tension and she'd be ill.

"Are you going to cook at uncle's house, Candra?" Roddy persisted between bites. "Will I have to work? Will we have to beg for our food and get locked in a basement?"

"Broderick! What an idea!" Candra silently wished she could slip under the table. Of all the people for him to be with when he allowed his already overactive childish imagination to run totally rampant, Roddy had to pick Josh!

"That's what happened in the movie on television when the little boy started stealing, remember? They sang and danced and had a lot of fun after he met the other boy, though, the one that was a pick-pocket."

Candra smiled in spite of herself. *"Oliver Twist,"* she informed Josh. "And Uncle Ted is too nice a man to allow that to happen. I'll be working as his secretary, not mopping floors. So enough of that. It's time you were in bed before you fall asleep at the table." And give any more information to Josh, she added silently.

Candra led the reluctant child to bed, putting off the time when she would have to face Josh without a buffer. Even though he was downstairs she was as aware of him as if he were standing next to her. She gave Roddy a drink, tucked him into bed and read him a story. Then, dreading the moment of rejoining Josh, she decided to go to her own room.

She paced, unable to sit or stand quietly. Why? Why? Questions kept popping into her already muddled brain. Why would Josh contrive to bring them both together like this, and after all this time? None of it made any sense to her. These past weeks had already taken their toll until she was hardly able to think straight, and now this!

The door opened without warning and Candra stopped her pacing and looked up, startled by the abrupt movement. Josh stood in the entrance. His face held an expression of implacable steel—lifeless, emotionless and hard. The air crackled with invisible tension as they faced each other, waiting for . . . what?

Josh broke the silence. "If you're through playing coward, come downstairs."

"I'm tired."

"At seven-thirty? What's the matter, Candra? Can't you face me alone after all these years?"

Candra took an involuntary step forward, her hands clenched into fists. "What do you want from me, Josh? An apology? An apology for something I did as a child? All right. Once more, I apologize."

"Stow it. I don't need it now. In case you haven't realized, I grew up too. I had to face up to what you did a long time ago. And after that I had to face the fact that you hid behind your father. Even after being confronted with the truth you wouldn't retract your statement. You couldn't face the situation."

"You're not worth facing! You're trash, just as you were nine years ago!" Her hand swept the room. "Who bought you all this? Which woman did you sell yourself to this time? When Bettina gave you that gold watch, did you decide you liked the taste of money? How does it feel to be a prime stud, an animal for hire?" She had lost control and aimed for the most vulnerable part of him just as he had done to her earlier. Suddenly she realized what words had passed her lips and in stark fear she watched the whitening of his face.

"You damned little witch!" he ground out, grabbing her arms to drag her against his lean, hard body. Josh's green eyes sparkled with diamond-hard hate and her fear began a shivering deep in her stomach that radiated throughout her body.

"What's the matter, Candra? Are you wishing you were the girl I supposedly made love to in the barn that day so long ago? Are you wondering what it would feel like to lie in my arms, have my hands on your soft flesh, caressing you, making love to you? Is that it?" He didn't allow her time to answer. His mouth came down hard to bruise her lips in a kiss that took her breath away. He tugged her closer still, molding her slim body to fit with his. Her anger had been swallowed up in fear, and now both emotions disappeared to be replaced by another feeling that was far more threatening to her senses—arousal. She couldn't fight him, even after she realized what form his punishment was taking.

His hand twisted in her hair before he cradled her head in his palm. Candra stood clinging to his shirt as the shock of his assault wore off to be replaced by a warm feeling that slowly unfurled deep inside, becoming more heated as his kisses turned softer, gentler. She moaned her frustration at battling her emotions and finally gave in to the overwhelming urge, clutching his shoulders as she moved her head to burrow closer to his, her body pushing in the instinctive movement of all lovers. Nine years vanished and once again she was the child who had loved him, who had silently suffered her crush on him.

Within seconds she was swirling in a sea of confusion. Josh had thrown her away, pushed her back onto the bed, a look of total disgust and contempt marring his features as he looked down the length of her body, before lifting his eyes to read the emotions playing over her face.

"Straighten your clothes and come back downstairs. Now that I know what you're like and what you're after, we'll strike a bargain." He turned and opened the door, glancing once more over his shoulder. "If you're not down in five minutes I'll come back up and get you."

The door shut and Candra gave a quivering sigh,

resting her face in her hands. How could he have done that to her? And how could she have responded like such a wanton? No one, not even Jamie, had ever gotten such a reaction from her. She had always been too cool, too emotionless, too composed, to ever allow anyone close to her. Until now. Candra placed a hand over her mouth, still feeling the pressure of his lips on hers. Was he right? Had she always wondered what his kiss would be like? Her mouth formed the word "no" but her mind said "yes" over and over.

"I must be going crazy," she muttered to herself, feeling the tides of so many emotions wash over her weary body.

When she got downstairs, Josh showed a stern face, the lines from nose to mouth deepening in his anger. He handed her a crystal snifter of honey golden brandy, then walked back to the fireplace, standing with one hand in his hip pocket, pulling his slacks taut across his muscled thighs. The other hand swirled the liquid in his glass as he stared into the brightly burning flames.

Candra clung to the thought that by tomorrow she would be gone. For now she would simply listen and keep quiet. He couldn't say anything she didn't already know and he couldn't hurt her more than she had already hurt herself.

"I want to apologize for that scene upstairs." His voice was low and raspy with just a hint of harshness as he continued to stand with his back toward her. "I shouldn't have done what I did, but so help me, you goaded me on."

"I know," she said tiredly, her bones suddenly aching with an unbelievable weariness not even sleep could dispel. How did a troubled soul sleep? "Tomorrow I'll leave you in peace, but until then, can't we declare a temporary truce? I know it's much too late, but I'm sorry for what I did to you. I can't correct it now, though, without raking up the past. I've never forgiven myself for it; I've lived with the shame. But . . ." Her voice drifted off and she glanced around the beautiful, expensively decorated room. "You don't seem to have suffered much for it," Candra halted, the words stuck behind the lump of tears in her throat, "while I've regretted it every day since."

She walked to the large bay window. The rain had turned to sleet again and the ground was shining in the early moonlight, giving the earth a clean, crisp sheen.

"Why?" Josh's voice broke into her thoughts as she turned, startled out of her reverie. He hadn't moved from his previous position; he was still standing next to the fireplace, staring into the flames as if they held the answer to his question. He raised a hand and tilted back his head to take a large gulp of the searing brandy.

"Why what?" She couldn't keep her eyes from the strength of his muscled shoulders. He had developed from a strong youth to a mature man, and a better specimen of manhood would be hard to find.

"Why do you regret what you did?"

She took a deep breath to calm her fluttering

heart. She was too tired to be having this discussion. She should be in bed, resting up for the tribulations of tomorrow. She sighed again. She had often wanted to confront him and apologize for her behavior, but no words could alleviate the anguish she had caused him. It was too late.

"It wasn't long before I realized just what I had done. I mean really realized . . . not just as a child, but as an adult. You were in trouble, then you left completely; Bettina and her family moved and father married so I would have a mother who could 'guide' me through the years ahead. We all suffered for my actions." Josh began to turn toward her slowly. "No! Don't look at me. It's easier to say this if I can't see your face," she begged and he turned to face the fire once again, his back rigid. She continued haltingly. "You were my moon and stars, the only stable thing I could cling to in those days. I was spoiled and selfish, but I needed your guidance, your time, your attention. But in that need was a fear of sharing, because I thought you would become lost to me. I was so selfish in my childish ways that I would rather have lost you than share you with anyone." She swallowed hard before continuing. "I know that's no excuse, but it's the only true one I have." His back remained turned to her, and she spoke once more. "I'd give anything to undo it, but I can't. It's too late."

The room was filled to bursting with silence. Suddenly a log shifted and sputtered and they were both brought back to the present.

"But you can undo it." His voice was a mere

whisper, but it echoed resoundingly through the large room.

"I don't understand." Her eyes searched his as he turned to face her, her expression showing her confusion.

He waved a hand to dismiss her question as he asked one of his own. "Are you going to marry Jamie Dieterman?"

Now she was really confused. Her head hurt and his question made no sense. "How do you know about Jamie?"

"I've kept track of the old crowd," he said dismissively. "Answer me."

"I . . . I haven't decided yet," she lied, without quite knowing why. Perhaps it was the small menacing smile that played at the corners of his mouth.

"Then you're not," he stated smugly. "Or you'd be making wedding plans instead of joining your uncle."

"We . . . we decided to give ourselves the summer to make sure it's what we both want." She lied again, suddenly feeling trapped.

He grinned, a slow maddening grin that made his green eyes crinkle at the corners and her heart beat faster in reaction. "Liar."

"It's none of your business anyway!" she exclaimed, angrily placing her drink on the end table. "I'm tired and I think I'll go to bed now, Mr. Laurence. I gave you my apology and you can take it or leave it. I'll be going in the morning, so you won't have to worry about whether I'm engaged or not. I doubt if the lack of that information would keep you up at night, anyway."

"I have a proposition for you," he said to her retreating back, stopping her in midstep. She slowly turned to face him, wondering just what he was going to say and wishing she had the courage to ignore her curiosity and keep on walking.

Curiosity won out. "And what sort of proposition would that be? I don't usually listen to the kind you're probably an expert at, so I think we'd both be wasting our time."

"Tsk, tsk, Miss Bishop, you're prejudging again. Your temper hasn't changed a bit." His mocking green eyes burned into hers and she could feel her skin flush a deeper red. But she stood her ground, not giving an inch.

"All right, Josh. State your case." She smiled sweetly, but it didn't hide the sting. "Or should I call you Scott now? You seem to do business under so many names."

He stiffened with anger and suddenly she wished she hadn't taken quite that tone. Her heart pounded heavily as she waited for him to yell, but he swallowed his anger instead. "Scott is my middle name," he explained as if to a child. "And after my run in with your segment of Portland society I found it easier to use it." His voice was distant and noncommittal, but his even monotone got across, more than shouting could have done, the depth of his suffering during that time so long ago. Regret for her hasty words filled her immediately and she murmured, "I really did make a mess of things, didn't I?"

She walked slowly toward him, stopping only when she rested her hand on his arm and begged for his understanding. "Please forgive me. It's never easy to be a child of thirteen, even under the best of circumstances."

Josh's dark green eyes stared down at her. His only concession was a short nod as he turned away, making her drop her hand. Apparently even her touch was to be shunned.

"Are you ready to hear my proposition?" he asked gruffly.

"Yes." Her head was bent in a gesture of contrition. She was too tired to do anything but acquiesce.

"You sold the house and the factory went on the auction block. And now you're on your way to live with and work for your uncle. Am I right?"

"Yes, you're right." She lifted her glass and took a sip of brandy, feeling the heat of the liquid slide down her throat. "But I'm not going to sponge off him, if that's what you think. I'm going to be working for our living. It was clear from the outset that it was what both Uncle Ted and I wanted."

"Is he going to pay you a salary?"

She sipped her brandy again, knowing she shouldn't have. Her head was spinning already. "I don't know. We haven't discussed it yet." Doubts began crowding in on her. What if he didn't expect to pay her? Would she be working for nothing, still begging someone for the things that Roddy would need to enter his new school in the fall? Would she be a charity case to an uncle who didn't even know her and might not want to?

"Will Roddy be staying with you?"

Spirit flashed for just a moment on her tired and drawn face. "Of course! Roddy belongs to me, wherever I am."

Josh nodded as if he had received the answer he expected. "Does your uncle's neighborhood have good schools? Are there any other children Roddy's age for him to play with? Will he be able to roam the woods, play ball, go fishing and all the other things little boys his age want and need?"

"I . . . I don't know." She felt the heavy weight of apprehension. Was she being too hasty in going to Uncle Ted's? She didn't really know him at all; she had only seen him once or twice that she could remember. But what else could she do? Her parents trained her to be the perfect hostess, but how much calling for that occupation was there? She would not let him see the doubts he had raised. Candra stood straighter, bracing her shoulders. She had intelligence. That should count for something. Besides, this was the chance she had always wanted. She would be on her own and could make a life for herself and Roddy that would hold meaning for them both. So why was she worried?

"Drink up," Josh ordered imperiously and she instinctively moved to obey, sipping the amber-colored liquid. It relaxed her almost instantly. The storm continued to brew outside, making the room seem a cozy haven.

"I seem to need a secretary for awhile," Josh said, dropping his bomb into the silence. His green eyes narrowed as he took in her shocked expression but he continued. "I need help and I can pay top wages immediately. And I'd enjoy having Roddy around. This is a good place for a child to grow up. There are horses and chickens and a few cows. A river that was made for fishing runs right outside our back door; we have good schools, nice neighbors and several other children his age live nearby."

"Are you serious?" Was this his idea of a joke?

"Yes, I'm serious," he said impatiently. "Unless the job seems below you." Josh glanced out the window at the storm, which continued to blow. "You won't be able to leave here for at least two or three days anyway. That's plenty of time to see whether or not you can handle the work load."

"But why?" Her voice was barely a whisper.

"Because I need help and you're here. Pepe is supposed to be taking care of the animals and helping with some of the renovations we haven't completed yet, but he's been so busy with things for me that he hasn't had much time to do anything else. You'd be able to take things off his hands." He hesitated. "You'd serve my purpose very well."

She had a right to be cautious. None of this made any sense, even to her befuddled mind. "Why offer this 'opportunity' to me? You don't even like me."

Josh shrugged, turning away and dismissing the question as he reached for a cigarette. He lit it and blew smoke between them. "Suit yourself. You're still going to have to stay for the next two or three days, regardless. This storm is a big one from all indications. We hardly ever get weather this severe in this part of Oregon, so the highway crews are probably unprepared."

"Please, I . . ."

"If you think I'm asking for a repeat of the star performance upstairs, let me put your mind to rest. That was anger, and I'm no longer angry. It won't happen again." A knowing grin spread across his sensuous mouth. "I have that problem taken care of, very capably, by someone else."

"A mistress?" At his nonchalant shrug her anger flared brightly. "A mistress!" she repeated scathingly. "If you think for one moment that I'd clean up after your mistress you've got another think coming!"

"My, my. Are you still so conservative in this day and age?" he murmured smoothly, completely unruffled by her vehemence.

"You're darn right I am, and I intend to raise Roddy the same way! He's going to have a normal decent home life, or as normal as I can make it. And that doesn't include mistresses!"

"Then I'll visit her elsewhere so I won't offend your delicate sensibilities," he returned mildly.

He had taken all the steam from her argument, leaving the embers to smolder just below the surface. Somehow it hurt more than she wanted to acknowledge to think of Josh with another woman.

"Go to bed, Candra, and sleep on it. We'll discuss it in the morning," he said softly, lifting the glass from her trembling hands and placing it on the table. "There's no rush." He turned her around by her shoulders, his touch sending small electric currents through her body.

She could feel his eyes on her as she slowly climbed the stairs. When she reached the top step she turned and looked down. He stood in the center of the room, sipping his brandy, his dark green eyes watching her through a screen of smoke.

"Good night, Candra."

"Good night, Josh," she answered, knowing that was all she was capable of as her feet dragged her toward the door of her room. There was just too much to think about and she couldn't cope with it all. In the morning she would be able to think, to reason out why he wanted her here at all. There had to be a reason.

4

Come on, Candra! Wake up! It snowed last night! Can we go sledding? Please?" Roddy bounced on the bed, his exuberance uncontained as he pleaded with his sleepy sister.

Candra placed a pillow over her head and moaned sleepily. "Roddy, how can you be so energetic after yesterday?" she grumbled as he pulled on her hand to gain her complete attention.

"All we did was drive in the car yesterday," he explained as if she were the child and he the adult. "But if I'd'a known it was going to snow I'd'a been happier yesterday!" The bouncing stopped suddenly as something struck him. "Candra?" he questioned hesitantly, and she knew from his tone of voice that he was worried about something. "Mr. Laurence acted like he knew us. Does he?"

"He used to work for Daddy a long time ago, punkin." Candra sat up and tossed her tangled hair behind her shoulders, watching his reaction. Suddenly she was wide awake. "Why do you ask?"

"I don't know. I thought I liked him until he was mean to you," the child answered honestly. "Do you like him?"

"I don't know him that well, Roddy. We'll see." She reached out and gave his small skinny ribs a tickle, making him fall back on the bed in a fit of giggles. "Now, scoot out of here so I can dress. I'll meet you in the hall in ten minutes. Ready or not!"

Roddy scrambled off the bed, his feet skimming across the floor as he ran for the bathroom. "I'll be ready before you are!" he exclaimed, undoing the buttons on his pajamas before he reached the safety of the bathroom door. The door slammed and she shook her head ruefully as an irrepressible smile tugged at the corners of her upturned mouth, her eyes softening with love for him. She was going to have to talk to that boy. Not everyone liked noise as much as she did, and if they were going to stay here . . .

"What am I thinking?" she exclaimed softly, stunned that overnight she could have come to such a momentous decision.

She pushed the pillow out of the way and sat up, wrapping her arms around her legs and letting her chin rest softly in the nest made by her knees. Her thoughts drifted to Josh. Had the years changed him? Once he had been a tall, well-formed youth with a ready smile and mischief gleaming in his sea green eyes. Even when she had behaved abominably he had exercised patience toward her. And now that she had grown up she realized just how much restraint he had used when she had indulged in one of her childish fits.

He had begun working for her father when she was just nine and he had been a father figure of eighteen. She had clung to him like glue from the very first meeting. And he had allowed it. In those days he was the brother she had never had, her mentor, her encyclopedia, her touchstone in a life that was at once lonely and yet filled with people. No one had cared for her like Josh. When she was thirteen and reaching for the promise of the young woman she would soon become, Candra had spied him with Bettina Wallace, their neighbor's youngest daughter, as they rode along the wooded path by the river bank. Trees dipped to cover them in a forest of cool shaded greens and a sharp knife had twisted inside her. Without knowing why, she had wanted to lash out at them both, hurting them as much as she was hurting. Later, when Josh had returned to the barn and was busy rubbing down the horse, Candra had done just that, yelling with a girl-woman temper she was unable to control.

"Don't you ever see her again, Josh! Do you hear? You're supposed to be working for my dad, not off in the trees with *that* girl!" she had screamed in frustration. But he had continued to calmly brush the animal's already gleaming coat.

"What's the matter? Growing up already?" His tone had been patronizing, fueling her anger even more.

"I'm grown up and I'd like to spit on girls like Bettina! She's nothing but a tramp; I've heard people say so! And you're no better than she is. You just take care of my father's horses, that's all. Besides, if her parents knew they'd have a fit! Maybe I'll tell them!"

He had gotten angry then, angrier than she had ever seen him. He stood tall, holding the brush in a knuckle-whitening grip. "Whatever Bettina does, Candra, is none of your business. If you say anything to anyone, I'll take a paddle to your backside until you can't sit down. Do you understand, little lady?" His voice had been low, almost calm, but the menacing undertone and the blaze of green in his eyes made her realize just how angry he was. "You can get me into trouble all you want, but don't ever hurt anyone else with your petty bouts of jealousy."

"I am *not* jealous!"

"Then what is this fuss all about?"

Before thinking she had blurted it out. "You're mine, that's what! And I don't want Bettina around you!" Tears had poured down her cheeks as she clung to his waist, hugging him tightly as if he would disappear. His arms had gone around her automatically, cradling her securely. He was her rock and her family and, strangely enough, she was the same to him.

"That's enough, Candra," he soothed. "No one's going to come in here and steal me away in the

58

night." His voice held a tinge of laughter, but it was also soft and reassuring. He placed his hand under her chin, lifting her face so he could see her tear-glazed eyes. "But, Candra, I don't belong to anyone. People aren't cattle or puppy dogs for others to own. People have feelings and wants and needs, just like you do, and it's unfair for you to try to set rules for them. Do you understand?"

She had nodded her head eagerly, needed his approval after his anger, and he had laughingly brushed away her tears. But she hadn't really understood. Not until later.

A sound brought Candra back to the present, and she shook her head to clear her thoughts. It would do no good to rake up the past. It was over. She climbed out of bed and walked to the bedroom window to stare at the scene below in pensive silence. The snow was still falling, swirled by the blowing wind, to form beautiful crystal patterns on the trees and window sill. The road would be impassable now, judging by the look of the drifts against the barn and fences. Josh had been right. It looked like she was going to be here for a few days whether she liked it or not.

She sighed heavily and reached for the pair of tan jeans and chocolate plaid shirt she had laid out the night before. She'd knot her tan sweater over her shoulders in case it was cooler downstairs. It was time to face the world . . . and Josh.

Persimmon place mats held bright lemon yellow plates and cheery white glasses filled to the brim with orange juice. Breakfast selections were laid out on the kitchen bar. Roddy had been too impatient to wait for her upstairs and was now busy making himself at home.

Josh was there too, looking altogether too well rested, she thought. "Good morning, Candra," he greeted her. "It's going to be lovely seeing your smiling face every morning," he went on with only a hint of sarcasm. "I'm glad that you and Roddy will be staying."

Roddy stared at his sister, his mouth widening into a grin. "Are we really, Candra? Wow! That's great!"

"Don't talk with your mouth full; it's not polite," Candra corrected automatically, not knowing what else to say. Josh had cut off her retreat by mentioning unsettled plans in front of Roddy and he knew it. Hoping her demeanor was calm, she faced the perplexing man next to her. "Before an agreement is reached, Mr. Laurence, I'd like to have a private word with you." His eyes narrowed. "Encompassing duties, wages, that sort of thing."

"Of course." He began eating from the well-filled plate in front of him. He was calm and unruffled, but somehow Candra knew he was secretly laughing at her. Damn the man!

"Ready?" He broke into her thoughts and she quickly swallowed the last of her coffee before reluctantly following him through the living area and through the door beside the fireplace.

He led her down a hall past two doors, pointing toward each as he passed them. "Utility room. Study." He stopped at the end of the hall in front of another closed door. "Bedroom," he said and Candra stiffened. But instead of entering he retraced his steps to the study. He opened the door and stood back, motioning her to enter.

Candra glanced at him through her lashes as she slipped past him, noticing the slight smile tugging at the corners of his mouth. He was once again silently laughing at her, this time at her reluctance to enter his bedroom. Her chin was held high and jutted out in determination. Her eyes were sending cool composed thoughts . . . she hoped.

The room was obviously a library. New and old books covered three walls, their haphazard sizes, shapes and colors crammed together, making it more cozy than any decorator could have done with regulation chic. The fourth wall was a floor-to-ceiling window that caught and framed the morning sun peeping through a dense thicket of tall pines like a brilliant life-size painting. A large and well-worn wooden desk stood in the center of the room and a tall grandfather clock ticked quietly away.

"Please sit down." Josh was being overly polite to irritate her, but there was no way she would allow him to get the upper hand.

"Thank you," she said, equally polite, primly sitting in a small straight back chair instead of the rather obvious brown corduroy wingback that sat across from the desk. She stared past his shoulder and toward the outdoors. The sun had broken through the clouds and turned the crusty snow into a brilliant white mirror. Suddenly a trapped feeling invaded her, making it hard to keep her outward composure. Every nerve in her body vibrated, warning her of an unfamiliar danger.

"I don't know how much of the house you've had a chance to see so far, but there are five bedrooms, four up and one down, along with three full baths." Josh hesitated, as if allowing her time to make a comment, but she continued to stare out at the pristine scene. "Pepe tells me the house is easy to keep clean, but it *is* time consuming, so I'll ask you and Roddy to take care of your own rooms." He glanced down at the top of his desk then back at her. "All letters, correspondence and filing are done in here." She turned to look at him and he sat down, picking up a pencil and twirling it absently as his eyes probed her. She knew he was trying to disconcert her, but she wouldn't let him. She turned to the window again. "Just like any other little boy, I want Roddy to have chores. It's good for children to be responsible for something besides themselves." He sat back and a smile tugged at his mouth. He had expected fireworks and he could tell by her expression that he wasn't going to be disappointed.

Candra bristled. "I see. And just what do you think Roddy should do in order for him to earn his keep?" she questioned, barely able to keep the irritation from her voice.

"He should be responsible for the trash, help Pepe with the animals, pick up after himself. That sort of thing." Suddenly he grinned, showing even white teeth. "What did you think I had in mind, Candra? Child labor laws have come a long way. I can't work him from sunup to sundown."

"I know that," she said stiffly. "It's just that you're supposed to be hiring *me*, not my brother. I would prefer to keep our relationship on a strictly professional basis. Besides, I still haven't decided whether I'm going to take the job or not."

"Yes, you have. You know just as well as I do that your uncle isn't all that keen on having the two of you with him. He only offered out of obligation. Is that what you want, Candra? To live with a relative on sufferance? Or would you rather get paid for your work and keep your integrity?" She began to speak, but he held up his hand to silence her. "And if you want to give me a story about Uncle Ted, you can forget it; I already know his financial position and it isn't very strong. He'd work you to death before he could afford to pay you a penny."

Candra suspected that he was right, and that thought hurt. But she couldn't allow him to know that. She stood, wanting to bolt and yet unable to allow her pride to bend. "Perhaps this job won't suit either of us. I've never been a secretary and you've never been a father to a small boy."

Josh stood slowly to walk around the desk and lean against its edge. She watched him as a mouse might watch the movements of a stalking cat. He folded his arms across his chest, flexing the muscles in his arms. Her eyes were glued to him now. What would it be like to feel those rippling muscles with her fingertips? How taut would his skin be if he was holding her close?

"Oh no, Candra." His eyes narrowed, watching the blush recede from her cheeks. "You may be right about my being a father to a little boy," his green eyes deepened in color, "but I played surrogate father to a young girl until she began to constantly remind me what a young lady she was growing into. So I do have some references for the job." His voice was as soothing as warm honey, catching her off guard. It seemed like eons before the implication of his words sank in.

"Is that what you thought of our relationship?"

He nodded his head. "At the time."

"I had a father, in case you've forgotten."

"And in case you turn him into a saint now that he's dead, I'll remind you how little he thought about you. The only time you got his attention was when you were in a scrape. Remember?"

"He cared. He just didn't know what to do with me. I was supposed to be his son, not a daughter who didn't even look like him. And when my mother died all I did was remind him of what he had lost." She stood and spun around quickly, staring at the grandfather clock through a haze of tears she wouldn't allow to fall. "He tried, but I was too young to understand and too impetuous to be patient."

Josh muttered an oath under his breath and his hands rested on Candra's tensed shoulders, drawing her back against the length of his body. She leaned against him, suddenly feeling safe while she was near him. A sigh slipped through her slightly parted lips.

His breath was warm against her neck when next he spoke. "And what excuse can you give your father for his behavior with the son he finally had?"

"You had to know Alicia to understand. Dad married Alicia right after . . . after you left. She was supposed to be the mother I had lost and the wife he had missed so terribly. But no one can take another person's place. We all found that out quickly enough. Alicia might have looked like my mother in the flesh, but she was as different as could be in spirit."

Josh's hands traveled down her arms and Candra melted against him, leaning her head back to rest on the warmth of his chest. Her eyes slowly closed to block out the rest of the world. For the first time in months she felt completely at peace with herself. This was where her heart told her she belonged.

But the initial calmness rapidly deteriorated into a sort of breathlessness. Her heart began a more rapid, primitive beating and her nerve endings tingled at the man who stood so closely behind her. A warmth began in the pit of her stomach, then spread, creating a dull ache that radiated through her body. She longed for something she couldn't understand and it frightened her. But when she tried to pull away Josh tightened his hold, not allowing her to escape from the viselike grip of his arms. She struggled for just a moment before surrendering to the tumultuous emotions he evoked, then fell back to rest her head on his chest once more. His warm breath fanned her cheek as he lightly kissed the tender spot on the side of her neck, sending shivers down her spine.

"What's the matter, Candra? Are you afraid you'll melt like warm sugar in my arms?" There was a hint of teasing in his voice. "That's certainly different from the little girl I knew who used to hurl herself at me from across the room. What happened to that little girl? Hmmmm? Who would have thought she'd grow up to be such a beauty, beautiful enough to tempt the most honorable of men."

He buried his head in her flowing hair, his kiss feather-gentle on the sensitive soft spot just below her ear. His hands left her arms to cup firm breasts, his fingertips softly teasing, tempting. Her heart skipped a beat, then settled into an even faster rhythm than before and she gasped, trying to make one final effort to draw away. It was unsuccessful and she slumped back, giving up the mental as well as the physical struggle. She wanted to feel his touch as much as he seemed to need to touch her. She could feel his rapid heartbeat against her back, thumping in erotic unison with hers, and reveled in her power to affect him as much as he affected her. She moved slightly to fit more closely against him and his already taut thighs stiffened further as he twisted her around to face him.

His eyes had turned a deep green, as deep as the sea, and they glinted with a passion she had never seen before. She lost herself in their depths. Then his moist mouth came down to claim hers with a fierceness that took her breath away and the world went spinning wildly off its axis, showering the heaven's stars against her closed eyelids. She held on to his neck and shoulders as if they were a lifeline.

When he slipped his hands down to her hips to mold her closer to feel the very essence of him, she gave a small moan, a sound that came from deep inside. She was totally yielding and confirmed it by wrapping her arms around his neck, burying her fingertips in the thickness of his hair. There was no will in her but his will. She was at his total mercy and she didn't even want to fight. He pulled her closer, but it was still not close enough to quench the flame within. His hands wandered over her body, exploring her secret curves as if he was claiming his own private treasure. He played with her senses, toying with her, teasing her into being the aggressor.

The fire of wanting grew deep inside, swirling through her body to create a deep-seated need that had to be assuaged. She moved against him, wanting him to take her, make love to her, sate her intense longing for him. She had never felt this way before. She wanted his hands to touch her, needed him to quench the burning sensations that he had aroused. No one had ever skyrocketed her to this height before. No one had even ignited a small candle of want, let alone lit this burning compulsion to throw everything to the wind in order to have what she so craved.

Her hands curled down to push and lift his heavy sweater so she could reach the faintly dampened skin and rough mat of hair on his chest. Her small nails teased his skin, begging him to respond as she did. He groaned, deepening his kiss further until they breathed as one. Still it was not enough for either of them.

"Let me make love to you, Candra," he muttered hoarsely. "I need you. Heaven knows, I need you."

His touch had a hypnotic effect on her senses, numbing her mind while her body had never been so in tune and alive. She nodded, keeping her eyes closed as his lips came down to claim hers once more. She gave herself up to the intense pleasure of his experienced masculinity, reveling in this alien feeling of submission. She was his and he wanted her. That was all that mattered.

When Josh pulled away she was bereft. His green eyes moved across her face from her passion-swollen lips to her blue eyes, dilated and heavy lidded with his lovemaking. He searched her for an answer, one hand finding the outline of her mouth, the curve of her brow, the line of her cheekbone. A small smile of satisfaction and triumph crossed his face before he took her hand and led her to the door.

"Where are we going?" The marvelous feeling of lethargy was leaving, to be replaced with an inner caution.

He gave her lips a quick kiss before opening the door and leading her down the hall. "To my room."

She was pulled into the darkened room just as the realization of what she was actually doing broke through to her fogged brain. She hesitated for a moment, her mind fighting to escape the fog of her body's sensual wanderings. She had never done this before and the taboo was strong in her. Josh must have sensed it, because when he reached the center of the room he pulled her into his arms once more, kissing her until she was too confused to resist. Again the compelling desire to consume and be consumed was the only thought that Candra had. She was swirling in a vortex of emotions so strong it took her breath away.

Josh growled deep in his throat, "Somehow I knew you'd be like this. I knew you'd grow up to be both beautiful and desirable, but I didn't realize how much." He murmured against the corner of her mouth, "Now I know. Now I know." The admission was given as if pulled from the depths of his soul and it thrilled Candra even before his lips claimed hers in a kiss born of intense wanting. "Touch me, Candra. Hold me."

Her arms wrapped around his waist, her teasing fingers playing a desire-laden tune as ancient as time.

"Do this," his hoarse voice told her, taking her hand to raise it to his chest and ruffle the curling hair between his own muscled nipples. "And this," he muttered, taking her other hand and pulling it around to press against his indented back.

"Tell me what you like, what you want, my Candra." She led one hand back down, imprisoning it against a swelling breast, murmuring her approval as he teased her. She was where she belonged, in the nest of Josh's arms. And he must feel the same way, she told herself, or he wouldn't be as impatient as she was for the culmination, would he? His heart couldn't beat this fast for just anyone. Only her, only her, her pulse beat answered, drumming the rhythm in her ears.

"Candra!" A small boy's voice wobbled through the door. "I cut my finger!"

Josh froze, then turned away.

"I'll be right there, darling," Candra called, turning her back toward the room and straightening her blouse.

She opened the door and took a look at Roddy's finger, which was barely scratched. Josh was right behind her, and he sent Roddy to the kitchen to find Pepe, saying, "I need to talk to Candra for a minute, half-pint."

As soon as Roddy was gone he pulled her back into his arms. "I'm sorry about that, Candra," he breathed. "It will be better tonight. No interruptions."

"There won't be any tonight, Josh. This was a mistake. A big mistake. Thank heaven Roddy interrupted and I was saved."

"Just a few minutes ago I would have bet that you didn't want to be saved," he retorted angrily. "At least, you didn't act like you did."

Candra's mouth moved but no words came out. Her mind was in neutral and she couldn't think of a retort. He was right; but the way she had behaved was totally foreign to her nature, even though he didn't know that.

His angry voice echoed in the near empty room. "We seem to have a very potent chemistry between us, whether we like it or not. Don't you think it ought to be explored?" His eyes searched hers for confirmation, but found confusion instead. The tears threatened to spill down her cheeks and she suddenly felt like a child again, but this time there was no one to comfort her. She certainly couldn't run into Josh's arms.

"I wonder if you're as innocent as you seem or if you're just a study in acting ability," he mused as if to himself, his eyes narrowing on her slightly parted lips and sparkling eyes. She stiffened. If that's what he thought, then, let him!

"I'm an excellent actress. Almost as good as you are when you're playing the injured party or the tender lover. But while I'm still an amateur, you're definitely a professional!"

She watched his square jaw harden in anger, his green eyes glittering like ice chips, and her legs turned to jelly.

He turned his back to her, as if dismissing her presence. "I wouldn't be too pleased with your situation if I were you. A sharp tongue can be curbed in several ways, none of which would appeal to you."

"Don't worry," she replied bitterly. "I won't be around long enough for you to 'curb' me, as you put it. As soon as this storm is over, I'm leaving!"

"That's fine with me. Meanwhile, I'll pay you to do what I asked of you. And when you're ready to leave, you'll have some money and I can be left in peace." He reached for a half-empty pack of cigarettes on the nightstand and lit one, blowing a smoke screen between them as he waited expectantly for her answer.

She wanted to throw his words back at him, but stopped in time. Why not earn a little money while waiting? After all, she was grown up now and this was just a job, like any other. Perhaps it would prove to him that she was no longer a vindictive child but a woman grown and matured.

Josh sighed as if tired of the entire scene, then

walked to the door and opened it to silently usher her out.

When Candra reentered the main portion of the house she heard Pepe talking to Roddy and the small boy answered with laughter. Everything was once more in order as far as Roddy was concerned. But what about her? She would never forget the mocking look on Josh's face as he opened the door. He had known all along that he had issued a challenge and, what's more, that she would accept.

5

Josh joined them in the kitchen a little later, but only to say that he was on his way to his silo-office to work. Candra was unable to look at him, simply nodding her head at his explanation. She didn't dare ask any questions that would focus his attention on her. She felt such a variety of emotions and they constantly fluctuated. Shame, because of the way she had so wantonly behaved in his arms with no thought of stopping. An almost awed wonder that Josh was able to stir in her what no other man had ever come close to rousing. And mixed with these the uncontrollable sense of destiny that of all the places she could be snowbound, she was here, with Josh.

Pepe gave her an overall idea of the way the house was run and where things were kept in case Candra

needed them. He explained about the multiline telephone and what she should expect while she was
working for Josh. And when she finally had enough
nerve to ask, he also explained about the silo. Josh
had bought the property about two years ago,
renovating it as business allowed and living in Los
Angeles when he was too busy to do anything but
work. The silo had been converted first, the bottom
floor turned into a gym, sauna and whirlpool bath,
while the upstairs was a round turret type office
where Josh did most of his work.

"Just what does Josh do, Pepe?" Candra asked
casually, more interested in Josh and everything
concerning him than she cared to admit even to
herself.

"All kinds of things," Pepe said vaguely. "Different
for each company. You'd better ask him. I don't have
much to do with that side of his life."

"Have you known him long?"

"Since he was twenty-two and came to live on the
Warm Springs Indian Reservation. He helped with
the livestock, then moved on to work timber." The
older man shrugged. "When he left, I left with him.
We moved to Los Angeles, then back to Portland,
then came here."

"Portland? When?" Had Josh been to Portland
since her father's death? It wouldn't serve any
purpose to know, but her curiosity was piqued. Was
that why he knew so much about her? Had he cared
just a little bit?

"I don't remember; a few years ago, I guess. We

didn't stay long." He closed up like a dark closet, his expression telling her that he would say no more.

"Do you enjoy working for him?" she asked softly, amazed that this impassive man held such a deep respect for his employer. His affection for Josh showed in his work, even when his expression was closed.

"He is my friend," he stated simply, turning to end the conversation as he set about stacking split wood on the fireplace grate in readiness for the evening fire.

Candra began her duties immediately, sitting down in front of the brand new electric typewriter. Everything in the house was the best that money could buy. Everything had been done with forethought and skill. Even the arrangement of the upstairs bedrooms, with the full bath in between, showed the care and planning that had gone into the conversion. And if she knew Josh even slightly, she would bet her last dollar that the ideas were all his. He seemed to be skilled in more than one area.

She smiled at her own thoughts as she opened the desk drawers to find paper and carbon for the letters Josh had left for her to type. Perhaps after she finished she would help Pepe with dinner, even do it herself. She had always enjoyed cooking and had often done so, especially after her father had died and Alicia had taken over the running of the factory. There hadn't been much money to do anything but keep up what Alicia had referred to as "appearances," and cooking was something no one saw or noticed as long as there was a maid to serve when the occasion warranted it. This would give her a chance to show her skills and prove a point at the same time. She was not useless!

By the time dinner was ready to be served that night Roddy was bathed and dressed in pajamas and a robe and Candra still had enough time to relax in front of the fire and enjoy a hot cup of spiced wine with Josh as he detailed the steps he had taken in renovating the barn. An unspoken truce had been made between them. He was cool and distant, but at least he wasn't scorning her efforts or making fun of her.

"Why didn't you have a crew come in and do it all at once?" she asked, curled into the corner of the soft couch, sipping her drink and enjoying the soft background music. The swirl of snow outside, the hiss of the blazing fire that sent shadows jumping all around the room made it cozy and warm. Even the muffled noise Pepe made as he set the table seemed intimate.

"Some of Pepe's friends came down and helped us until we had the outside in shape. But once it was sealed and weatherproofed and the inside walls were up I wanted to do the rest of it myself." Josh sounded as if he were talking about writing a letter instead of the major undertaking Candra knew the construction had been. Not everyone could turn an old barn into a new home almost single-handedly.

Candra tilted her head, looking over the rim of her glass, and Josh's grin deepened intimately, sending her heartbeat into double-time as he answered her unspoken question. "I enjoy working with my hands. I find it relaxing, like jogging or playing tennis would be for some people." Then he turned the tables. "And what about you? What have you been doing these past nine years besides getting into gossip columns by being seen by the right people in the right places?" His smile became tinged with frost and hers disappeared as she felt suddenly bereft of his warmth.

Her voice was tinged with sadness as she answered, remembering how bored she had always been in that particular crowd. Had everyone judged her by the same yardstick that Josh had? She supposed so, but that didn't help the hurt.

"That was Alicia's idea of the right thing, I'm afraid." It wouldn't have been such a lonely life if she had been allowed to do something else to while away the empty hours between social engagements. But Alicia had never permitted it and Candra had been afraid of making too much fuss for fear that her stepmother would take her resulting anger out on Roddy. Or, even worse, on her father, whose heart was already giving signs of the massive coronary that would claim his life. "I've taken care of Roddy," she said simply, not realizing how much insight she had given Josh with that remark.

His green eyes narrowed as he contemplated Candra's expression. She only seemed to become animated when she spoke of her brother.

She continued slowly, as if Josh were not there and she was musing alone. "At first, when Daddy died, I did nothing. It was the shock, I guess. Alicia

had told me the company was in temporarily bad
straits, but she never intimated that things were as
bad as they were. I think she wanted me to marry
money so I could continue to support her in the style
to which she had become accustomed." An overwhelming sadness brought tears to her eyes as she
saw what her life could have been if Alicia had been
different.

A log crackled in the fireplace, sending out a
shower of sparks. Suddenly the silence was overpowering. "But what about you?" Josh questioned.
"Do you miss the lifestyle that Alicia loved before she
killed herself in that Porsche of hers?" His voice was
casual, belying the intensity of his gaze as he waited
for her answer.

She continued to stare into the fire, afraid to show
him what was in her eyes. He was doing strange
things to her and she couldn't bear to see his
contempt for her feelings. "No. Not at all."

"That's hard to believe."

"Why? I've told you that I learned a lot since I was
a child. Why is my changing and growing so hard to
believe?"

"I don't know." He sipped his ruby-colored wine.
"Sometimes the past is impossible to forget." His
tone was flat, as if he were talking about the weather,
or worse, about someone he cared too little about to
give much thought to.

She stared at him, willing him to say more, but
when nothing came she spoke. "I want you to know
how sorry I was, Josh. I was just a child playing
grown-up and I failed miserably. I hoped for years

that I'd see you again, accidentally, so I would have a chance to explain. Then, after a while, I hoped I *wouldn't* see you, because I was so embarrassed," Candra explained candidly, staring at him unwaveringly.

Josh slowly turned toward her, returning her stare before sighing deeply and glancing into the depths of his glass. "At first I was angry and hurt. I thought you had betrayed me, that we had had a better relationship than that. Then bitterness replaced the hurt because I was forced to move from a place I considered my home." His eyes were empty of emotion. "And now I should be thankful to you. If that hadn't happened I might still be a stableboy and not where I am today."

"And where is that?"

He motioned vaguely. "Here."

"Which is . . . ?" she prodded.

"I'm like a holding company. I have interests in a lumber mill, a recording company, various other things." Josh stood abruptly, ending the conversation and leaving her wishing she knew more about this enigma of a man. "Is dinner ready?" he asked Pepe, who nodded and smiled in return.

Candra uncurled from her cozy position. She'd wait. Sooner or later her curiosity would be rewarded. She didn't want to delve into the whys and wherefores of that curiosity, but she did want answers. She stood and stretched; her eyes caught Josh's and for a long tense moment their gazes held. She could tell by the darkening of his eyes that she affected him and an excited thrill ran up her spine.

The blood flowed quickly through her veins, making her almost dizzy. Then, suddenly, the bond was broken and Josh turned away, a look of disgust on his face.

"Do you work at being provocative or is it something that comes naturally?" His caustic barb hit home. She *had* tried to be provocative. She wanted him to be as aware of her as she was of him, yet she couldn't explain her reasons. A blush worked its way up her neck to tinge her cheeks and her embarrassment was complete.

Candra had fixed stuffed pork chops with buttered and parsleyed potatoes, along with green beans lightly sprinkled with slivered almonds. A crisp salad livened by tomatoes and radishes accompanied the meal, with chocolate pudding for dessert. Josh simply assumed that Pepe had prepared the meal and Candra refused to tell him otherwise. What did she care, she asked herself, whether he knew or not? *She* knew, and that was the only important thing.

They finished dinner in companionable silence, the truce having reasserted itself, lazing over coffee and cigarettes until Candra noticed Roddy's tired eyes filling with sleep. But like all small boys he was unable to give in to the sandman willingly.

"Will you read me a story, Candra?" he begged when she told him to head for bed.

"I'll be up in a few minutes, darling. Let me help Pepe clear the table." She rose gracefully and picked up the plates and scattered silverware. "Meanwhile, choose a book you want me to read. There are a few of your favorites tucked into the box at the foot of your bed." She looked at him and gave a soft smile.

Roddy returned a tired smile before walking toward the stairs, his feet dragging across the polished floor. He had helped Pepe with the animals that afternoon and the exciting but unexpected rigors of farm life had completely tired him out. Josh rose in a single fluid motion, reaching for the remaining dishes and bringing them to the bar. "Wait a minute, pardner. I'll read you a story while your sister helps clean up."

"You will?" Roddy's eyes grew round in surprise. Candra swiveled to face them both, wondering why he was so willing to allow Josh that nighttime privilege when it had always been their own special ritual. She pushed down a sharp twinge of jealousy. Roddy needed more male companionship, so why was she becoming so possessive? She hadn't thought anything of it when he spent the afternoon with Pepe. Roddy glanced at her for confirmation and she swallowed hard, nodding her head and smiling encouragement with more enthusiasm than she felt. She didn't notice Josh's eyes taking in the pallor and indecision written on her face.

Josh and Roddy walked up the stairs together, Josh's hand on the small boy's shoulder, and Candra deliberately turned her back on the hearttugging picture they made. They looked like father and son. It should have been her father instead of Josh who walked Roddy up the stairs. A lump formed in her throat and she turned quickly to begin doing the dishes, scrubbing at the plates as if wiping the scene from her mind. Closeness, tenderness, love—all that was for other families, not for her and Roddy. They had no security, no love, except each other's.

She had offered to let Pepe get on with his other chores, so she was alone in the kitchen, staring out the window. The snow had a frosty covering of crisp ice. The pristine scene brought back other memories, long hidden, of cold winter nights that held the same qualities of peace and wonder. Long ago those evenings had been spent in the barn with Josh, nursing an animal or fixing a faulty piece of equipment. They usually wound up sitting on bales of hay stored in one of the stalls while they sipped hot chocolate and talked. Josh would tell her of the Indian reservation where he had spent a summer and she would tell him of her mother, her fears, her dreams of the future. A lonely girl, she had poured out her whole heart to him.

Candra could suddenly feel the straw beneath her feet and a hot mug of cocoa warming her hands as she sat beside Josh, listening to him play his most recently composed song on his scratched old guitar. She was almost thirteen and the whole world was inside the barn doors, wrapping her in friendly comfort.

"When I grow up I'm going to marry you, Josh," she had said decisively when he had finished his new ballad and placed the guitar on the bale of hay next to them.

He had laughed, a deep rumble that filled the air. He bent and ruffled her already mussed hair. "Not me, Candi. I'll let some other poor man be driven wild with your tantrums. I'll just sit back and laugh."

"But don't you want to get married?" she had questioned innocently. "You're so old now, why are you waiting?"

"I'm twenty-two and I wouldn't call that old. I want plenty of time to see the world and taste its sweetness before I settle down with a wife and a brood of kids."

"My brood."

"No, Candra," he had said, more serious this time, his green eyes trying to tell her what she couldn't absorb from words. "Not yours, sweet. You're something special, or will be when you grow up, and I'm just your daddy's hired hand. You'll find someone special someday, just watch."

"But I want you!" she had exclaimed heatedly, attempting to wash away his doubts with her own positive feelings. Her will would make it come true!

He had just shaken his head, smiling sadly at her lack of understanding, refusing to argue with the boss's daughter. Why had he bothered with her? she wondered. No one else had. No one had given her the understanding that he had volunteered. She leaned against the sink counter and heaved a deep breath. Was it because they had both been lost souls? Had they each made the other into the family they had wanted so desperately? Given each other the security of knowing someone cared?

"Are you a thousand miles away because you don't like it here?" Josh murmured in her ear, breaking her reverie, and she glanced up sharply, seeing the two of them reflected in the window pane. Her body responded to his nearness and she gasped at the strength of her feelings.

"I was remembering the time I proposed to you." Her voice was husky, her candidness unexpected, if the startled look on his face as it was reflected in the window was anything to go by.

"In the barn? I remember." There was a smile in his voice. "In the same breath you told me I was old." His mouth tilted up at the corners and his eyes crinkled in a smile of remembrance.

"Tell me, Josh. Why were you so patient with me? Why did you take time away from your own youth to help me, listen to me?" She twisted around to face him and he took a step back, as if wary of touching her body with his. She noticed the action and her heart plummeted. So he still didn't want to be near her, to touch her. But her glance was unwavering as she gazed into his deep green eyes, waiting for his answer. "Tell me, Josh. Why were you so patient with me? Just like you are with Roddy?"

His answer came slowly. "Because I think I needed a family at that time in my life and you supplied it. Now that I'm older it doesn't negate the fact that I know how lonely it is for a small boy to be alone . . . even when he has a doting sister." His words were almost whispered, but they were firm in their conviction and a feeling of safety enveloped Candra. She had known he was understanding and caring all along. His words only confirmed her original thoughts.

He seemed to think he had shown too much of his

personal side and tried to cover up his real feelings. "I'm a sucker for strays." He grinned. "Someone has to take care of them."

"I never knew anything about your parents, Josh. What happened to them?" She tilted her head back to look into his face, her eyes searching, looking for the answers to questions that had long roamed around in her mind.

His warm breath fanned her cheek as he answered. "I was an orphan. I ran away from more welfare homes than you can count. Finally I ran away and they didn't find me. I bummed around until your father hired me and I made my home with him."

Candra took a deep breath, smelling the tang of his aftershave mixed with the clean smell of soap and that indefinable smell of man. It was a heady aphrodisiac. "I'm sorry. I didn't know."

"There's a lot you don't know, Candra." His voice was low and husky and it aroused her senses, rasping a response from her tautened nerves.

"Tell me. Help me understand, Josh," she pleaded, her eyes large in supplication. "Why were you so kind to me today? You offered me a home and a job. Why?"

"Don't read too much into people, Candra, or you're liable to be hurt when their answers don't match your expectations." His voice sounded cold, but his eyes were turning a darker green and Candra felt drugged with a momentary power. He wanted her! She could see it in his eyes. He wanted her.

It was as if a thin thread wound around them to

bind them together in the dim light of the kitchen. They were in a world apart and didn't need words to communicate any longer. Their eyes spoke the volumes they couldn't say. She longed to reach up and pull him close, but knew instinctively that he would pull away if she did. He was the male animal and he had to do his own stalking.

"Really?" The tip of her tongue caressed the outline of her lips provocatively. His eyes watched its movements and his breath escaped in a hiss. She stood completely still, waiting for the moment she craved when her lips would be crushed by his, her body touched by his. She could envision them wrapped in each other's arms, his mouth teasing hers, his touch heating the fire that already sped through her veins. Suddenly he turned and walked toward the door, leaving her chilled by his sudden self-control.

"I'm not here to appease your curiosity, Candra, just to tell you that Roddy is waiting for you to come say good night." He looked back over his shoulder. "So you can quit the act. I must admit, you're an even better actress than I gave you credit for earlier, but then, years of working at any craft are bound to make one better at it."

"I wasn't acting!" she defended herself, dismayed that he could think so badly of her. His back was toward her as he walked through the kitchen door and over to the stereo, turning the sound just a little bit louder.

A cry strangled in her throat. She wanted to kick him, force him into awareness of her. An unreasoning anger shook her to her very toes. She clenched the counter with all her might, allowing the sharp edge to cut into the softness of her palm. Finally the intense emotion receded enough for her to at least look calm once more. Then she carefully made her way up the stairs, head held high and trembling hands clenched. She would *not* give him the satisfaction of losing her temper in front of him so he could once more call her a child. She walked toward Roddy's room, her back ramrod straight. Never had she been so humiliated! But a little voice laughed in the back of her mind. She had also never been so excited, so alive as when she was with him. She opened the door of Roddy's room and walked quickly to his bed, placing a kiss on the already sleeping child's forehead. Without another sound she walked through the bathroom and into her own room. Closing the door quietly, she walked calmly to the bed, pulled down the bedspread and grasped the pillow in both hands. Silent tears coursed down her cheeks as she slammed the pillow against the mattress again and again before dropping in an exhausted heap in the middle of the bed.

6

Candra awoke to another brisk morning of snow. The storm had not yet abated and she wondered just how much more snow was going to fall. It looked deep and pure white, like a warm covering for the earth. A feeling of peace washed over her as she stared out at the beautiful landscape until she remembered the scene from last night.

She had cried a bucket of tears, burying her head in the pillow to muffle the sound of the sobbing that came from so deep within. Strangely enough, when she awoke this morning there were no aftereffects. Her eyes didn't burn, her throat didn't hurt, her muscles didn't even feel sore. It was odd. She hadn't cried since her father's death; she certainly hadn't shed a tear over Alicia's. Not even when the house was sold and the factory went on the auction block had she broken down. But last night . . . last night one man made a few cutting remarks and she had fallen apart like a china doll.

She shivered. That scene had hurt more than anything she had endured these past months. Her chin rose determinedly. But it wouldn't hurt anymore. She'd get dressed, pack up Roddy's things and they'd eat. Then she could check on the car. After all, it couldn't be that hard to change a tire, snow or no snow! She heard Roddy downstairs, his laughing voice carrying to her ears. How long had it been since she had heard that sound? Alicia hadn't liked noise in the house unless it was of her or her friends' making. In her opinion, children were neither to be seen nor heard. When Candra's father died she had expected things to change, expected that Alicia would suddenly become the mother that Roddy so desperately needed, even more so now that his father was gone. But it wasn't to be. Guests came and went in the same profusion as before, barely breaking for the funeral and the following few weeks of mourning.

Candra slipped into her jeans and a cashmere camel-colored sweater. She applied mascara, a touch of lipstick and a slight dab of rouge to hide the pallor of her face. By the time she was dressed the entire house smelled of biscuits and bacon.

Roddy and Josh were in the kitchen, while Pepe was gathering wood outside. Roddy was carefully counting out cans of water to add to the pitcher of frozen orange juice, his small hands attempting to hold the can steady as he made the trip back and forth from pitcher to sink. His grin grew wide as he spotted Candra standing in the doorway.

"I'm helping, Candra!" he proclaimed delightedly, holding aloft an empty can. "See?"

"You sure are," she answered, holding back a smile and fighting an almost overwhelming urge to hold him tightly to her. Her eyes met and locked with Josh's. His eyes crinkled in the corners as he slowly grinned, the movement making dimples in his cheeks as he searched her face.

"He's learning to be a bachelor. All men should know their way around a kitchen, don't you agree?" he teased. It was as if last night hadn't existed. Her own eyes glistened mockingly as she gave him her unspoken message. *You may have forgotten what you said, Mr. Laurence, but I haven't.*

He received it loud and clear and the light seemed to die in his eyes as he continued to beat the eggs in the blue-speckled bowl.

"It seems very logical to me." Candra walked up behind Roddy and leaned over his shoulder. "But don't you think I could help? I can cook too, you know."

"In that case, be my guest," Josh intervened, his voice cool and distant. "A woman's place *is* in the home. In every room."

"Including the kitchen, obviously."

He shrugged his broad shoulders. "If that's where she wants to be. I had another room in mind, but . . ." He let the sentence dangle, his green eyes flashing a message she couldn't misinterpret, and she blushed. She wasn't used to verbal fencing with men . . . at least, not this kind of fencing with this kind of man!

Breakfast was eaten quietly. Roddy was too busy filling his mouth with food to notice the tension in the air and Candra deliberately ignored it, calling upon all her resources to act cool and calm. He would not win this round, she told herself; he would not! Then he would glance up and her eyes would lock with his and all her newfound resolutions scattered while she became lost in the warmth of his smile.

Josh stretched, reaching for the rafters as he leaned back in the chair, his lean muscled thighs straining against the dark fabric of his slacks. "Very good. Looks like our stomachs aren't in jeopardy. Wait until Mrs. Jackson finds out that we survived without her."

Candra glanced up quickly, her heart skipping a beat. Until this moment she hadn't realized just how much she wanted to be here and that in itself was dangerous. She hoped her tone of voice was casual. "Who's Mrs. Jackson?"

"She's my housekeeper. Right now she's staying at my apartment in L.A. while she visits with her family. She'll be back in another two weeks. Pepe and I decided we could handle things here for the time being and let her have a much-needed vacation."

"I see." Relief flooded her. For a moment she had thought . . . Never mind, she told herself. It doesn't matter, because Josh is not for you. "I'd like to check on my car today and see what needs to be done to get it into working condition," she said quietly as Roddy scooted off his chair and carefully balanced his plate in two small hands as he made his way to the kitchen sink.

There was a small pause before Josh answered, as if he were choosing his words with care. "Of course, Candra. But you know you can stay as long as you wish."

She raised one haughty brow. "After last night I would assume that we aren't compatible." Her hands clenched in her lap, wrinkling the starched white napkin she held. "And I'm not about to be anyone's whipping boy because of a past that I can't rectify." Josh's eyes widened in surprise, then darkened with an emotion that was quickly hidden. She almost gasped at the change.

He stood stiffly, carefully sliding his chair back into position. "You're absolutely right. There's nothing that either of us can do to change the past," he replied tersely. "It's time for me to go to work. I have some letters on the tape player in the study. If you need anything, call me. I'll be in the silo."

All that morning Candra concentrated on the work at hand; business letters to various companies that Josh held at least a part of, or in some cases owned completely. She told herself that there was no point in trying to fix the car with the weather the way it was, but that she would certainly find a way to leave in a day or so.

Lunchtime came quickly—soup and sandwiches. The table was only set for two, but Candra wasn't surprised when Josh tramped in from the silo, his forehead furrowed in a frown. She couldn't explain why, but she had known that he would return before dinner. She quietly made another place for him at the table, neither catching his attention nor looking at him. By the time Pepe served lunch and they had eaten, Roddy's eyes were closing as he leaned on the table, one small elbow rocking as it held up his head. Candra's face softened as she smiled at her little brother, love for him shining from her eyes. It was definitely time for a nap.

Josh's change of attitude from last night was perplexing. He ignored her, but an almost tangible awareness bound them invisibly together. Could that be the reason for his abrupt about-face this morning when he had smiled at her as if they both knew the same secret? Her outward coolness matched his, but she couldn't deny that the blood flowed faster through her veins when he was near, or the pulsing in her throat as his eyes came into contact with hers. She took a deep breath, letting it out slowly so he wouldn't guess just how disturbed he made her feel.

Just then she glanced up to find him looking intently at her. Candra's eyes were as cool as his were obviously puzzled. She raised one brow in question, hoping her calmness would irritate him, but he only shrugged as he took another bite of his roast beef sandwich. Was there a hint of a smile tugging at his mouth? Her irritation rose as she watched through her lashes for any other sign of laughter. She could take almost anything, but she would *not* be laughed at!

"Very good," he murmured as he rose from the table and carried his plate into the kitchen.

She decided to keep the atmosphere light. With a little luck she would soon be gone, and if she behaved herself they could part as distant friends. "Pepe does a good job of cooking, doesn't he?" she forced herself to say with a smile aimed somewhere in the vicinity of his shoulder. She thought she detected an answering smile, but refused to look directly at him to find out.

Within a few minutes Josh had gone and she had settled Roddy upstairs in his bed. The house suddenly seemed quiet and totally empty. She straightened the kitchen, since Pepe was outside, and slowly walked around the living room. Without Josh's inimitable presence the room was as hollow as she felt. She stopped her quiet pacing in front of the stereo and looked through the carefully organized cassettes. Almost all of them were labeled in a neat hand; only a few had commerical labels. Had they been recorded at Josh's studio? There was no answer. She marveled at Josh's orderliness as she took one out and slipped it into the machine. The music filtered softly through the room, encasing her in its melody.

A sultry-voiced female singer began a mournful tune, singing a haunting melody that Candra dimly remembered as a hit from about two years earlier.

The words seemed to have a message for her, upsetting her more than she wanted to admit.

> *Yesterday's dreams of long past*
> *Haunt my todays and tomorrows.*
> *Yesterday's dreams of long past*
> *Overshadow all my sorrows.*
>
> *All the ifs and maybes cannot change what*
> *was*
> *And all the ghosts of dawn give pause*
>
> *Yesterday's dreams are lost*
> *In memories that mold my tomorrows.*

Candra recognized the singer as Joan Macy, a blond-haired siren with a slightly gypsyish look. She was young, beautiful and could turn the worst lyrics into poetry. In this case however, no such transformation was needed. The melody and the words were beautiful even without her expertise.

Candra curled up in one of the large wingback chairs that flanked the fireplace, her slim legs curled under her. As the melody washed over her she realized just how much the lyrics pertained to her. Yesterday's dreams were just that—memories, and all tied up with Josh. He had wrung more emotion out of her in the past two days than she had ever given out in her life. At least, since she had seen him last, she amended. It seemed that whenever he was around she began building sandcastles for him to smash. She might as well face the fact, if only to herself, that his love was the one thing she wanted most and also the one thing that would always be denied her. She could only be hurt by Josh, but now she wasn't a child anymore, but a woman, with a woman's wants and needs and capacity for pain. Her own wants had gone out of control yesterday and frightened her more than she cared to admit.

She would have to be on the lookout not to fall into that trap again. She shook her head in dismay. Two days ago she had been worried that Josh was out for vengeance and now she was worried about getting into his good graces! She was insane! He had made his contempt for her plain from the moment she had arrived.

The piercing ring of the telephone broke into her silent reverie. It hadn't rung all morning, so why did it have to start now, when Pepe wasn't here to answer it? She stared down at the offending instrument, trying to recall all the directions Pepe had given her on which button did what, but nothing came to mind. She picked the receiver up and placed it next to her ear, her voice barely above a whisper as she answered. "Hello, Laurence residence."

"Laurence residence?" a female voice questioned brittlely. "Where's Scott? Who is this?"

"Mr. Laurence is busy right now, but if you leave your name and number I'll have him call you," she said coolly. She knew there was a way to buzz Josh in the silo, but the buttons on the phone were impossible to figure out on such short notice. Besides, who did this rude woman think she was?

"Who are you?" the high brittle voice demanded.

"I'm Mr. Laurence's secretary." There! Let her chew on that for a while!

"Secretary! Where's Pepe? Just what are you up to? What are you doing there?" The voice shot up an octave.

"I have it, Candra. You can hang up now." Josh's voice filtered over the line, cutting short any thoughts she might have had of continuing the conversation with the mystery woman.

"Yes, sir," she said in her most professional voice, a smile tugging at her mouth. If the woman was a mystery to her, at least she had the satisfaction of knowing that she was the same to "Miss Screech." The smile disappeared as quickly as it had come. Josh must be involved with the woman; she must be the mysterious mistress. There had been a strong note of possessiveness in her tone. Candra stared at the brightly lit button on the telephone; he was still talking to her. Suddenly the light went out and her heart skipped a beat. It hadn't been a long conversation after all. It couldn't have been more than two or three minutes from the time that Josh picked up the phone. She grinned and her heart felt light. She didn't want to know why she felt this way; just reveling in the feeling was enough for the moment.

She went upstairs to check on Roddy, drawing the afghan away from his small face and giving his cheek a light kiss. Then she ran into her room to run a comb through her hair and add a little lip gloss to her already pinked lips. Back downstairs, she stepped into the small passageway that led to the silo. Her emotions were topsy-turvy, her heart beating faster than it had ever done before. Would she ever be immune to the thought of his presence? Why did the thought of Josh's absence from her life hurt so much? She knew why, but she didn't want to face that fact. Not yet.

The passageway that led to the silo was done half in warm walnut paneling, half in glass, with a deep red Mexican tile floor. At the end of the hallway she found a closed door and knocked in a staccato rhythm. There was no answer. Taking a deep breath, she readied herself for a confrontation and turned the knob. The large round room was about fifty feet in diameter. Well rubbed cedar walls hid the built-in fluorescent lighting. The room was obviously a gym, with weights, a rubdown table, bicycles and other equipment. In one section was a couch with a single pole lamp and table. On a dais was a large square whirlpool bath in deep blue tile. Gabriel Manor had never been like this!

"All the comforts and then some," she murmured to herself in awe. Josh's interests certainly brought in enough money for him to live very, very comfortably. He had come a long way from the kid who groomed horses for a living and had grown into a highly complex man in the bargain; too complex for Candra to understand.

Lighthouselike stairs hugged the walls to the high-ceilinged room, ending at another door that she presumed led to his office. Slowly she walked up the winding staircase, her hand trailing on the slick wood of the banister. When she reached the top she knocked again, in the same fashion as before. He had to be in there. There was nowhere else, no other door.

"Come in," he barked and she pushed the door open, her heart beating like a triphammer. She shouldn't have come up here. She should have waited until dinner. But it was too late to back down now. She was here.

The room was the same size as the one below, but this one was completely enclosed with glass from hip level up. A large stereo system was built into the shelves under the windows, with cushioned seats under others. A large desk faced a perfect view of the cliffs and rapidly flowing river below. Tall trees, willows, fir, oak and pine, grew in shaggy groups below, the snow touching their branches like white icing on a Christmas cookie. Snow fell gently, accenting a perfect silhouette of Josh as he stared out toward some unknown object, his body taut and still. Even though his back was to her Candra knew that he was angry. Was it with her or with his caller? A giant black grand piano stood in the center of the room and she walked around it with trepidation to stand silently by his side, her hastily-thought-up excuse for coming temporarily forgotten.

Candra's legs trembled, a reaction she couldn't define. She suddenly felt like Daniel bearding the lion in his own den. Her large blue eyes dwelled on his stern profile, noticing the tightness around his mouth and jawline.

"I would have forwarded the call to you, but I forgot how to use the phones." Was that her voice that sounded so calm and cool? "I hope I didn't mess up your call."

The stiffness left his body as he let out a deep sigh. "It doesn't matter. I was expecting it; it was just a matter of time."

"I see," she murmured, not really seeing at all. What was he talking about?

"This looks like a recording studio," she said, for lack of anything more sensible.

"Does it?" He was distracted. Silence hung in the air like a heavy mist before his attention once more returned to her. "Look out there, Candra. See the edge of the storm? It will be over in an hour or so at the most." He pointed to the horizon. Dark clouds hung overhead, while the horizon was becoming a wide ribbon of brilliant blues. "You should see the view when the weather is right and the sun is setting. It's alive with colors that float all through the room, bouncing into your eyes to blind you with their brilliance." His voice was as deep and powerful as a physical caress, and Candra shivered in reaction. Then, as if he had said too much and showed more of himself than he had wanted, Josh reached for a glass of whiskey that sat on the desk next to him. He took a giant swallow, making the ice tinkle noisily against the crystal, underlining the tenseness that hung in the air.

Candra continued to stare at the horizon, her unseeing eyes blinking back the tears that threatened to spill down her cheeks. What had happened to her? What was wrong? What had she done to deserve this pain?

"Josh?" she questioned softly, laying her hand on his tensed arm. He turned quickly, opening a small cupboard that held everything for drinks, including an ice maker.

"Join me in a drink?" he asked casually and Candra could feel him making a conscious effort to put some space between them.

"Yes, please." She turned and continued to stare out the window. He had rebuffed her overture. He had rebuffed her.

"Scotch?"

"Fine. Water and ice, please."

The tinkling of ice in the glass warned her that he was now standing behind her and her breath quickened.

"Where's Roddy?"

"Asleep. He's worn out from his morning with Pepe and the horses and chickens." And I'm worn out from trying to guess what you have on your mind that you won't tell me, her inner voice explained.

"He needs a set routine."

"And he'll get one when he gets to my uncle's house." Candra sipped her drink, but she hardly tasted it. Josh was filling all her senses.

"Not that again. Are you telling me that you're turning down my offer of a job in favor of working for your uncle?"

"Your girl friend doesn't seem to like my position here and I learned a long time ago not to interfere in others' relationships. It was a hard lesson, but I never forgot it." She prayed he'd deny that the woman was his girl friend, but she knew he wouldn't by the expression of his face. "I'd be a fool to stay."

"I don't think Joan has much to say about the situation. I need help." He pulled on his drink once more, turning away from her.

"I think she does. Is she the mistress you spoke of earlier?" The words almost caught in her throat, but she had to know.

"Joan Macy is a singer."

"Joan Macy! Is she your mistress?" Candra persisted.

Josh finally faced her, turning slowly so that the sunlight played over the planes of his face. She longed to run her hand along his jawline, feel the texture of his skin beneath her palm, touch the chiseled outline of his lips with her fingertips. He was beautiful. He was every woman's dream. And he belonged to someone else; it showed in his eyes. A ball of pain grew in her stomach, searing her with more vengeance than she could ever have imagined.

"Candra . . ."

But she had her answer, and suddenly she didn't want to know any more. "There's no need for explanations, Josh. Too much has happened between us for you to owe me an accounting. But you were right about one thing. People are loaned, not owned. Funny how I never understood that until now." She turned slowly and set her glass next to his, then walked to the door. Her chin was in the air, her back straight as she tried to make a graceful exit. But it was not to be.

"Damn it, Candra! Stop being so dramatic and come back here," he ordered harshly, his patience obviously at an end. She halted, but did not turn around. "Your exit is wasted on me. I've seen the same old movies."

"I'm not acting. I just don't see any reason for you to explain something that's none of my business." She placed one shaking hand on the doorknob, holding tightly as if it would hold her up. "We've both been embarrassed enough by this reunion. I'll be leaving in the morning. Thank you for your hospitality, but I'm sure you'd have done the same for a stray dog," she ended bitterly.

"Pepe changed your tire yesterday, but the spare needs to be fixed before you set off. Or are you foolish enough to risk driving without it?"

Candra hesitated. "I'll have it fixed at a garage on the way."

"No, you won't. Tomorrow I'll take you and Roddy to Gold Beach and get it fixed. While the garage is working on it we'll go sightseeing."

Candra turned to face him then and was shocked. His eyes drank her in like a thirsty man tasting water and she thrilled to the unspoken message. But his voice was rough when he finally broke the tense silence.

"Are you going to argue with that, too? You always did try to run things."

"Is that so different from the way you behave? Don't you try to manipulate others? Aren't you trying to manipulate me right now?"

"Perhaps, but I always have a reason for what I do. You go off helter-skelter, bent on what you want whether it's good for you or not."

Candra's shoulders slumped. No matter what she said he would have a comeback. There was no winning with Joshua Laurence. No winning at all.

Josh poured himself another drink, then held hers out to her. This wasn't his usual habit, she was sure. What had put him under such an enormous strain? She sipped her drink and smiled grimly. She could have asked herself the same question. She hated Scotch.

Josh watched her closely as the late afternoon light brought out the blue highlights of her hair. Slowly his hand reached out and slowly he took her drink from her, placing both their glasses on the desk, his eyes never leaving hers. He pulled her into his arms, pressing her to his lean hard body. He held her still against him, his face buried in the softness of her slim neck, breathing in the sweetness of her skin. His touch was light and sure, his breathing deep and suddenly contented, and her heart sang in response. They were molded into one beautiful sculpture where there had been two incomplete ones. They belonged like this . . . together. Just feeling the firm impression of him against her made everything else a dream. This was her reality. All her doubts and fears flew away and would stay away as long as she was with him like this. His hands moved slowly over her spine to rest lightly on her hips before pulling her even closer to him. She went willingly, loving the touch and scent of him, needing it as she buried her head against the heavy throbbing in his chest.

"Candra, Candra," he murmured as if reciting a chant. His lips touched fire wherever they traveled, his hands were gentle on her skin, but seared it just the same as if they were tongues of flame. They wandered freely from her hips to the soft curves of her breasts, teasing, savoring the fullness that bloomed with his touch. Everything he was, everything he did, excited her to a pitch of forgetfulness. Her senses were finely tuned to his clean musky scent, the feel of his roughened fingertips as they moved across the nipples of her breasts. Even the taste of Scotch mingled with the warm moistness of his mouth was a highly erotic stimulant.

She knew the depth of her own emotions for the first time. She was drowning in her feelings for him. She would always love not just his body, but his soul, his thoughts, his habits. The high-handed way he had when he thought he could read her mind and tried to keep a step ahead of her, the way he raked his hair back from his forehead when he was irritated. She loved it all, his very essence.

Candra opened her eyes and bent back in his arms to see his face, her hands cupping his determined chin and loving the feeling of his slightly raspy beard in her palm. "Josh?" she queried, leaving the rest unsaid.

He understood her unspoken question and his eyes warmed, melting her with his look before he once more possessed her lips in a kiss that left nothing unsaid. His mouth drew on the sweetness of hers; his lean hard body instantly responded to the softness of her form. Her entire body sang with the wonder of her love. He had to feel the same way! He had to!

"Look," she whispered huskily a little while later. "The storm has stopped."

"Not in here. It's just begun."

His hand slipped under her sweater to find and cup one tender breast, his thumb moving over the tip to cause an all-encompassing tingle that poured all through her veins like softly flowing wax.

"You don't know just how lovely you are, darling. You're a temptation even the devil couldn't resist." His voice sounded like a growl, but his hands were gentle as they brushed the offending material away. He kissed her eyelids, closing them to everything but the exciting sensation of his touch, and she succumbed readily. She was trembling by the time he gently picked her up and walked to the long seat under the window, placing her there tenderly, as if she were a rare and priceless piece of art. His eyes traveled over her body, seeking the pleasure points that were within his vision, his need of her showing in the tautness of his body, the clenching of his jaw, as he stroked the skin beneath his hand.

Within seconds he was beside her, his lips, hands and long, strong legs touching her everywhere, soothing her heightened nerves. He shivered above her and she stroked his back, trying to reassure the man she wanted more than life itself. She was both the seduced and the seducer and it all came as naturally as breathing. An ache inside her began to grow and grow and she instinctively knew that only Josh could ease it. She moved, pressuring him to end this yearning that seemed to begin so deep inside her, and he rocked with her, making it worse.

"Easy, darling. Easy. It will come in time, I promise," he murmured as he nibbled on her ear. Still his hands stoked the fire in her as he slowly undressed her and there was no release. The ache was turning into a pain, a pain that needed release. It was frightening; she was at his mercy and he would not be merciful. He was a tyrant and a lover, giving her both pleasure and pain.

"Please, Josh. Please," she moaned aloud and his answer was to kiss her hard. He moved away for a moment to slip out of his clothes. Then he was back. His body positioned itself, then entered, slowly trying new territory and loath to hurt the trusting woman beneath him. It was over in a flash, with only a slight resistance to tell him it was the first time for her. Soon they were moving as lovers do, with the experience of a million years and the knowledge of a lifetime.

Candra hadn't known that love could be so beautiful, but when she cried out with a groan that began from deep inside her Josh's answer was a deeper echo of her own.

Their bodies were entwined together, damp from the efforts of love. Josh's hands never ceased their movement over her silken skin. He stroked her, settling her down after a wondrous experience that he knew was new to her. She lay in his arms, trusting and loving, still dazed from the depths of emotion he had known how to pull from her and her eyes continued to glisten as she stared up at him wordlessly. Her hands, too, still stroked him, his bronzed skin and firm muscles that rippled in the afternoon light. Her mind couldn't form a coherent thought; her mouth couldn't function unless it was to mold itself to his. In the span of an hour he had changed her whole life.

"No more hiding behind maidenly modesty now, my sweet," he murmured in her ear, his tone holding just a hint of laughter. When she stared into his eyes she saw a spark of mischief there, but also there was still a distrust, a reserve that even their lovemaking had not erased. Candra was suddenly still, her mind churning with chaotic thoughts. Her hands stilled, her body tensing. Did he care about her? Did he love her? Or was she just another woman to him?

"If I hid behind 'maidenly modesty,' Josh, it's because I have a strong feeling that you think I have none," she said quietly. "I know you brought me here, but I don't know why, or what you hoped to gain by it. You've given me no explanations."

He stiffened and it took all her control not to wrap her arms around his neck and hold him to her.

"If you think I maneuvered you, then you must think I'm some sort of a god. I didn't arrange a snowstorm or your flat tire."

"But you did arrange to have me bring those papers. Why?" she persisted softly, knowing that he was retreating from her, but unable to stop herself from pressing him.

He hesitated for a moment. "I wanted to see what

kind of a person you had become. The years had made me curious." His hands left her body and she was suddenly cold. The feeling that she had spent her life trying to deny was back again, but this time it hurt more than she could ever have imagined. It had been her father's rejection she had first felt, then Alicia's, and now the culmination of feelings that had been a lifetime raveling and knotting was in Josh's rejection.

She didn't know what to say, but she was saved the trouble of thinking of something when the telephone rang. Still lying beside her, Josh reached for the phone.

"Hello?" Was it her imagination or did he sound angry?

She couldn't hear what the other voice was saying, but she knew that it was a male. Josh answered in monosyllables until the voice at the other end changed to the light lilt of a woman. Candra's heart fell as she watched him absently run a hand through his dark hair, then tug at one earlobe as he listened to whatever the other party was saying. "Yes, all right." His back was turned, leaving her in no doubt that it was a personal call and that he would have preferred privacy.

She stood and put her clothes on, then walked slowly across the room, retracing her earlier steps. She reached the door just as he said, "All right, Joan. I'll see what I can do, but things are a little hectic here at the moment."

Candra stepped out the door and ran down the steps quickly, suddenly in a rush to get away so she could pretend that nothing had happened to mar their budding relationship. But something had happened, a little voice told her. Something profound and deep and she could never be the same. Had it affected Josh, too?

She remembered what he had said about being a very good actor. Was that what he had been doing until they were interrupted? Acting? Did he love her, or only want her?

Tears burned her eyes. Everyone had wanted her for different reasons . . . and they were all the wrong ones. Even Jamie, the man she had almost been engaged to at one time, had wanted to marry her only because of the money his family had needed. Had Josh wanted her simply to warm his bed and keep his correspondence running smoothly without interfering with his lifestyle? Her already taut nerves jangled at the question, telling her no. But common sense came to the fore to whisper a decisive yes.

7

The fire danced and leaped in the dark-bricked cavern, highlighting the bright brass screen. It was mesmerizing. Candra sat curled on the couch, two cushions away from Josh. She could feel his presence as she sipped her wine and stared into the flames, but she wouldn't acknowledge him.

Pepe had cooked and served dinner in his usual quiet manner, disappearing after he and Candra had cleaned the kitchen. Reluctantly she had put Roddy to bed, then joined Josh downstairs. It was going to be an uncomfortable evening for both of them, but she was unable to come up with a good excuse for not returning to the living room without looking like a fool. The striking of the large myrtlewood grandfather clock echoed from the study, drawing her attention to the time as she counted the moments before she would be able to excuse herself and retire to her room.

An almost unbearable tension filled the air, but Candra couldn't think of a thing to say to break the silence. Her nerves were already at the breaking point. How long could this tension last without one of them exploding with it?

"Candra." Josh's voice broke through the quiet, startling her, and she almost dropped her wineglass. Her eyes darted to his, then back to her glass again, as she silently acknowledged his bid for her attention.

"This has got to stop. You realize that, don't you?" His voice was low, harsh, vibrating with an emotion she didn't want to define even though her own heightened senses gave her the answer.

Candra took a sip of wine to steady her nerves, playing for time. "What do you mean?"

"I mean that this attraction we have between us is becoming impossible. You can't even speak to me and that's crazy."

"You mean I've upset your way of life? Your routine?"

His brows drew together, his green eyes turning stormy in the firelight. "That's not what I meant at all and you know it."

"What do you want from me, Josh?" Her blue eyes reflected the confusion she felt over her own chaotic emotions.

"I don't want anything *from* you. I just want you."

Candra's eyes widened with his blatant statement.

He acted as if he were discussing the weather! "What did you say?" she croaked, her voice little more than a whisper.

Josh leaned back, his eyes once more drawn to the fire. "You heard me. I want you. By tomorrow night. In my bed. I want to make love to you again."

"Am I supposed to get undressed this minute or should I finish my wine? Do I strip slowly or should I just throw my clothing off in my 'eagerness' to be with you?" she asked sarcastically, her hand trembling with the effort of holding the glass instead of throwing it at him. Anger had replaced all other emotions.

A slow tantalizing grin spread across his handsome face, making her want to hit him all the harder. "That's why making love to you is so wonderful, Candra. You're so volatile. That cold, sophisticated charm you exude is only a cover-up for a very passionate woman." He hesitated for a moment, his eyes devouring her. "I ought to know."

She set the glass down with a snap, then turned to face him, her own expression completely frozen. "I realize that you believe this conversation is flattering, and in a sense I *am* flattered. But the answer is no."

After a moment of stunned silence Josh threw back his head and laughed, a deep resonant sound that only fueled Candra's indignation. Several minutes passed before he could stop laughing and begin explaining.

"I'm sorry, Candra. I shouldn't have done that." He was still smiling as if she was a foolish child and he had just indulged her!

"I don't see anything funny about what I said," she retorted stiffly.

"I know you don't, but stop and think about it for a minute. Ever since you walked into my house you and I haven't been able to keep our hands off each other, no matter how hard you try to deny it. I didn't have to ask you into my bed; all I had to do was take you in my arms and in a few minutes you were ready to give me what I wanted without my asking." He leaned forward and she suddenly realized that the space between them had narrowed. His hand came up, one knuckle brushing against her cheekbone as his thumb sensuously rubbed against her bottom lip. His lids were heavy with desire, but his control was much better than hers. While she quivered under his touch he sat still and composed.

"But I want you to come to me of your own free will. It must be your decision, yours alone. I want you to need my touch, to want me to hold you close, to want me to make love to you just as much as I want to. I want you to want to explore my body as much as I want to find the hidden curves and delightfully sensitive spots of yours." His voice worked as an aphrodisiac, soothing and exciting her at the same time. "Making love takes two people, Candra, not just one, with the other lying passive. I want us to experience the heights of lovemaking . . . together."

"Why?" she whispered.

"Because the act itself is meaningless unless both parties are totally involved and pleasured by it."

"No." She cleared her throat, her eyes still unable to break with his. "I mean, why me?"

"Because there's more to us, to our relationship, than the past. Let's explore the present. But I want some type of commitment from you before we go any further."

"And coming to you as an aggressor is making a commitment?" Heaven help her, he was beginning to make sense.

Josh nodded slowly, his thumb now drawing circles at the base of her throat where her erratic pulse could be felt beating lightly against her pale skin. "It would be for you. I don't believe you're the type to bed-hop, my Candra. So a commitment of that kind from you would be total."

"Why me? I'm certainly not experienced, not the way you are."

He chuckled and it was a deeply intimate sound, meant only for her to hear and respond to. "If I wanted a woman with experience I'd have no problem finding one. What I want right now is you."

He moved toward her and she couldn't move away. He was the flute and she the cobra, hypnotized by his seductive music. His lips took hers in warm possession and she melted against his form, her arms wrapping around his neck to hold him closer. He teased the length of her body, his hands slow and teasing in their touch. His arms tightened, molding her body even closer to his lean male form. She clung to him, holding him, touching the soft springiness of his hair. One hand touched the strength of his jaw and his day's growth of beard rasped against her skin, making him a more sensuous reality than a thousand mental pictures. If he

115

asked her now she would have no choice but to say yes. All doubts fled her mind like birds on the wing. She was his.

Josh pulled away with reluctance, sighing raggedly as he straightened up, and she felt the bitterness of his withdrawal.

His eyes blazed a trail over her kiss-swollen mouth, then down her slim neck to her breasts, which kept rhythm with her fast breathing. He branded her with his searing look. "Like I said, I want you to come to me completely willing. I want you to know what you're doing, not allow me to kiss you into something you wouldn't normally do." The firelight shone on the angled planes of his face. "I want your commitment for our present."

Her blue eyes were still dilated with his lovemaking and she couldn't think coherently. She shook her head to try to clear it, but it didn't help. He spoke again, but this time his voice seemed distant. "You are responsible for yourself and your own actions. I want you to make this decision."

Those words hit her like a dose of cold water and she stiffened. "Count on the answer being no, Josh."

"We'll see," he replied, standing, then reaching down to the hands that were now clenched in her lap and pulling her up to him. "But meanwhile, I think you'd better get some sleep . . . alone. We'll leave tomorrow morning around ten o'clock and drive your car down to Gold Beach so the tire can be patched." His eyes narrowed. "But I want your answer tomorrow night. No matter what."

Candra didn't remember walking up the stairs and

into her bedroom. When she woke from her trance-like state she was standing in front of the window, tears silently streaming down her cheeks to dampen the collar of her sweater. Night shadows danced on the ground, etched clearly by the full bright orange moon. She felt like one of the shadows, moving constantly, but with no substance, no anchor.

She was constantly making resolutions and now she had made another one. While she was here she would have no more than a light, businesslike relationship with Josh. Hopefully she'd be able to leave without her heart being torn to shreds. With that decision made, she felt better almost instantly.

Roddy had a runny nose when he woke, but the excitement of going to town with Josh banished any complaints he might have been thinking about making.

They left right on time. Josh drove, with Candra next to him and Roddy in the back seat. The little boy's eyes darted in all directions; he couldn't see enough. The road was smooth, the sun warm and the snow was turning to slush.

"The last snow of the season and it clings as if it hates to give way to spring," Josh murmured, his smile devastating as he turned toward her. Obviously she was going to get the full quota of charm today as he tried to sway her answer.

She smiled grimly in return. She was determined not to give in to a man who wanted to use her just as he used his mistress. She had been vulnerable all her life, especially to him, but she refused to set herself up to be hurt again. She had no idea that her expression had changed until he spoke.

"Why so solemn, Candra?"

She turned to look out the side window, not wanting him to read more into her expression than she could control. "I was thinking that this is still such wild country," she lied.

"You're right about that. There's still a cougar or two living in the forests around here. Of course, you aren't allowed to shoot them unless they attack you, but you can still find tracks occasionally."

"Really, Josh?" Roddy exclaimed, half-excited and half-frightened, his eyes searching through the woods on either side of the road.

"Really," Josh mimicked, smiling to take away the sting. "I saw one once while I was visiting a family a few miles down the river from us. He sat in the yard and calmly groomed his fur, with chicken feathers sticking out of his mouth like a beard."

"What happened?" Roddy's voice was hushed.

"The owner went out and fired into the air. He was trying to frighten the cougar, but I think he was more frightened than the cat was. The cougar just stood up and walked back into the forest, wagging his tail slowly."

Both Candra and Roddy laughed at this description and no matter how hard Candra tried to keep it up, the flimsy wall she had erected around herself began to crumble.

Gold Beach was a small rustic town at the mouth of the Rogue River where it emptied into the deep blue of the Pacific Ocean. Once, when Candra had been very young, her father had brought her here on a business vacation. He had worked most of the time, but when he was free they had wandered up the coast to Agate Beach, where beautiful agates could be found in raw form. They had spent a happy day there before they had once more headed back to Portland and home, and fallen back into the stilted relationship her father seemed to prefer. On occasion, just before his death, Candra had seen the same warm glow in his eyes she had seen during that day spent on the beach. She had wondered then if he was sorry that things had deteriorated between them; she thought she could almost see the regret on his face.

"Where did you go?" Josh's voice was soft, bringing her back to the present. She turned and gave him a dazzling smile, but one that was tinged with sadness.

"I was remembering a vacation I took with my father years ago. We spent the day at Agate Beach." She turned away again and resumed staring out the window.

"A vacation that lasted only a day?" he murmured.

"It was combined with business. We were here for five days." She glanced back at Roddy, who was still looking out the window. He was undoubtedly scanning for cougars.

The drive was short; only thirty minutes passed before they pulled into a large gas station and mechanic's garage. Josh left the car and spent several minutes in discussion with someone in the shadows. Candra watched him for a while, then twisted around to look at the main street. It was a lovely old town with one street that paralleled the coast. There were none of the garishly bright department stores that cities had, but it was obvious that everything one needed to live comfortably could be acquired here. Beyond the stores on one side of the street Candra could see the deep blue of the Pacific as it melted against the shore. On the other side she had but to look over the buildings and she could see the beginning of the dark green forest, a little piece of heaven.

Josh's door opened, startling her from her reverie. "The tire will take a while, so I thought that Roddy might enjoy a small trip upriver. Hank, here," he nodded toward the older man standing behind him in greasy overalls and a wide knowing grin, "says his brother-in-law Sam is getting ready to deliver a package upstream. Want to go?"

Candra had no choice in the matter, for Roddy was already whooping his approval. Within minutes they had unloaded the flat tire and were driving across the large new bridge that spanned the Rogue River.

When they reached their destination, a small run-down dock with an even more dilapidated boat shed, Candra looked quickly from Roddy to Josh, her concern written on her face.

"A dock and an old building don't make a boat, Candra. I promise you it will be a safe trip," he said evenly, reading her mind. Then he smiled slowly in reassurance and her heart melted under the warmth that beamed from his deep green eyes.

Sure enough, the small power boat was new and shiny red, and the driver, a young man of about twenty dressed in jeans, a plaid flannel shirt and a sheepskin vest, seemed to know how to handle the vessel. He readily agreed to take along a few passengers on a trip that had long ago become routine for him. After placing a rather large package in the seat next to him and lashing it in, he started the motor and slowly steered the small craft up the river.

The wind gusted as the boat continued to run against the current and Candra pulled up the hood of Roddy's coat, making sure he was adequately covered. He didn't seem to notice her ministrations as he caught sight of a doe with large gentle eyes on a rise overlooking the river. Most of the snow had melted, though a few crusts of ice remained to dot the landscape. They came upon a clearing and saw cattle scattered over the untilled land before the forest once more moved into view.

Josh pointed to a huge rock that was covered with trees and the bright beginnings of spring flowers. "Elephant Rock!" he shouted over the sound of the motor. "A schooner came up here over a hundred years ago and people landed on that rock, carving the date on it."

She nodded to say that she understood. Roddy stared at it as if trying to figure out where the elephant was.

Sam pulled to the right side of the river and

steered to a small makeshift dock, cutting the engine and untying the package. "Be right back," he shouted over his shoulder as he climbed the embankment and headed toward a well-worn path that creased the incline. To Candra the silence seemed deafening, just the lap of the water against the boat and the shrill screaming of the sea gulls echoing in the valley.

"You forget there are places like this when you live in the city," Candra whispered.

"It is primitive country." Josh glanced around as if seeing the landscape for the first time. "I keep forgetting just how wonderful it is until a stranger comes along and allows me to see it through his eyes."

His words deflated her. He could have brought anyone along on this trip. Then his hand moved to cover hers where it rested on the side of the boat. "But your eyes are brighter and clearer than anyone I could have picked, so it makes the trip doubly perfect."

Candra smiled brilliantly; as far as she too was concerned the day was indeed perfect.

Within minutes Sam was back and they began the journey back downstream to Gold Beach. The trip took only half as long as it had earlier, because the current helped to speed them on their way. Twenty minutes later they climbed into the car and headed back to the station to pick up the repaired tire. Once again a black mood settled on Candra as she realized that she no longer had any excuse to avoid leaving.

They ate lunch at a local coffee shop, then piled back into the car. Josh drove along, his mind occupied with things other than his passengers. Roddy was keeping an eye out for cougars, looking from left to right every few minutes. As he scanned the landscape hope and just a little fear were written on his small face. Candra glanced at Josh, her heart flipping over at the sight of his strong profile. His face could have been carved from granite, it was so expressionless.

Pepe had already begun dinner preparations by the time they arrived home. Candra let herself be talked into playing one of Roddy's favorite games with him before it was time to eat.

The game board was spread on the carpet in front of the fireplace, with Roddy and Candra on the floor beside it, throwing the dice to see who would start. All through the game Candra and Roddy teased each other and by the time the game was winding up Roddy was winning and crowing about his sister's bad playing. She took it all in stride; the distraction had helped her to relax more than anything else could.

All day long the thought of going to Josh, being in his arms that night, loving him as she could love no other, had filled her with a strange sort of terror mixed with an almost intolerable level of excitement. Her mind constantly screamed "no," but her body craved the hands that would warm her, the lips that could caress her into oblivion. And the strain of her silent struggle had done nothing but confuse her to the point of exhaustion.

A noise at the door caught her attention and she

glanced up to see Josh leaning against the jamb, his arms crossed and an indulgent smile on his face. "Still can't win at games, Candra?" he teased.

She forced herself to grin back, shrugging her shoulders. "You used to tell me I couldn't think far enough ahead. I denied it at the time, but I believe it now."

"Your turn, Candra!" Roddy chimed, the excitement of winning glowing in his dark brown eyes. Candra smiled, ruffling his hair, then took her turn. Roddy rolled once more and the game was over. He whooped in delight as he made it across the finish line, leaving his sister's token halfway down the board.

Candra stood gracefully. On the floor she was without weapons against Josh. At least when she was standing she could almost meet him eye to eye. She glanced at him, warming when she realized that his eyes were glittering with a message she knew she interpreted correctly.

"All right, Roddy. Put the game away now and wash up for dinner," she said quietly, hoping that Josh would stop staring at her if she ignored him, but it didn't work.

"Is something wrong?" she asked coolly after Roddy had run upstairs. His easy smile disappeared to be replaced by a frostily mocking grin, one that she was fast becoming familiar with.

"Just watching the hired help." He walked toward the small bar and poured himself a Scotch and water. "No ice cubes," he muttered. Candra walked stiffly toward the kitchen, got out the ice trays and filled the ornate ice bucket that stood on the counter. As she turned a gasp escaped her. Josh was directly behind her, caging her in.

The moment was frozen in time, filled with an almost electrical tension. He held her arms and tightened his grip as they stared at each other.

Candra had to break the spell. "I didn't think you drank this early in the evening." She tried to ignore the tingling nerves that only stirred when he was near. He was too close for her to be rational.

"I drink when I want to." He brushed her small talk aside, his green eyes searching her face. She had never seen him look so vulnerable and her heart reached out to him as his look dissolved the already crumbling walls between them.

"I want you to make that decision tonight, Candra. I want you to come to me. Will you?" His hands tightened, hurting; but she hardly noticed. "I know it's not fair of me to press you, but will you come to me of your own free will, not knowing what I offer, except myself?"

Her traitorous pulse rate quickened at the thought of once more being in his arms. Where was that resolution she had made?

"Why, Josh?" she managed to say.

"I'm going to admit something and lay myself open for your scorn, but I think it's the only way for us to begin." He took a deep breath and leaned against the back of the counter, pulling her into his arms. Her body stiffened at the contact, but she was forced to lean against the strength of his chest, feeling the ripcord hard muscles of his thighs and the tautness of his stomach. His hands rested on the swell of her hips, making delicious contact as they smoothed the line of her shirt tail. "I've thought of you ever since I left your father's house. Even as I built a new life for myself, I kept track of you. But as I grew up, so did my imagination. You promised so much, Candra. I don't even think you knew your own potential, but I did. Now I find out that you thought of me, too. Don't you think that ought to be explored?" His hands cupped her neck, his thumb rubbing sensuously against her cheek and across her lips. "The damage has already been done, but it was at *my* instigation. Now I want it to happen again at yours." His mouth widened in a mirthless grin. "If you show up at my door this evening, then I'll know your answer."

"And if I don't?" she whispered, almost afraid to hear his answer.

"I'll know your answer then, too." He pushed her away, reluctantly but firmly, and turned toward the other room. "Either way, we'll both know the commitment we feel for each other."

He left the room silently; Candrā watched him while the ice cube trays dripped in her hand. But the ice wasn't half as cold as she felt when she thought of making the decision Josh wanted. How could she go to him, knowing there were no strings attached, and give herself to him the way he wanted her to? She loved him. She knew that without any doubt. She had always loved him and, in a sense, that love had been the basis for her cruel actions of so very long ago. She also knew that no one and nothing would ever be able to quell the aching that her love left inside her . . . except Josh himself. Should she give him that chance and open herself up to all the hurt that her declaration of love might bring? All her life she had wanted love and had never received it from anyone except Josh and now it was her turn to reciprocate. But could she do it?

Her emotions seesawed back and forth. Suddenly she realized that she still held the ice and she moved to put it away, glancing at her watch as she did so. It was five o'clock. She had at least five hours in which to make up her mind. She didn't even know why she was vacillating, when her body told her that being in Josh's strong arms again would be a slice of heaven itself.

Fleetingly she wondered where she had gotten her puritanical ways, but she already knew the answer. She had seen the bed hopping that went on in Alicia's crowd and then in her own. Her common sense told her that nothing was worth having if everyone could possess it. The idea of giving everyone the gift of oneself made the gift cheap. So she had kept away from casual affairs, even though her friends thought her odd for doing so.

By the time dinner was served she had regained her calm exterior. She never met Josh's eyes if she could help it, looking instead at the tanned column of his throat where the dark hair curled just above the open neckline of his shirt. At first he tried to draw her into conversation, but he soon gave up as he watched the color recede from her cheeks at his every word. Finally he said nothing at all, even to Roddy.

By the time Roddy was in bed Candra's nerves were once more at a heightened pitch. She had read three books to him, each sillier than the last. His eyes had closed before she finished the last story, but she continued anyway, stalling for time before she had to go downstairs to spend the rest of the evening with Josh. He had said all he was going to and now would await her decision. There were so many questions that buzzed around in her head. Why was he pressing her for a decision now when he had already tasted the first sweetness of her body? Why the rush when they didn't know each other any better than they had two days ago? Questions continued to pour over her in a continuous torrent, but only Josh held the answers and she wasn't brave enough to ask him. Not yet.

Finally Candra stood and stretched her cramped muscles, then put the book back on the shelf. She might as well stop delaying the inevitable and return downstairs. She closed Roddy's door quietly and walked to the top of the stairs, but she stopped short when she saw Josh looking up at her from below, a deep green light shining in his eyes. He spoke to her soul with that look and Candra's heart sang with the message. He loved her! No one could look at a woman that way and not love her. She smiled slowly. Now she knew what her answer would be.

She went down a step, her body and mind tuned to his every silent wish. Josh opened his mouth to speak, moving to meet her halfway.

"You've decided." It was a statement, not a question, and she silently nodded, a small shy smile playing around her lips.

He sighed, taking her into his arms and holding her with infinite tenderness. A few moments passed as they enjoyed the silent communication.

She placed her hands on either side of his strong face and looked into his eyes. "I'll change and be down in a few moments," she said huskily. "Why don't I meet you in your bedroom?"

Now it was his time to be silent as he nodded, reluctantly allowing his arms to fall to his sides as she turned and slowly retraced her steps to her bedroom. She glanced over her shoulder once, giving him a provocative look that made him start toward her before he caught himself. Then he turned and walked toward the back of the house.

Candra flew up the steps and into her room. Rushing almost frantically, she pulled the only nightgown worthy of such a night out of her closet. It was a pale peach and made her skin shine with hidden color. The straps were small and thin, the bodice snugly fitting to mold and lift her breasts, the skirt fell in small pleats to her toes.

She took a quick shower, powdered herself with her favorite scent and slipped into the gown. An almost unbearable excitement flowed through her, making her cheeks bright with color, her eyes sparkle. She glanced into the mirror and quickly gave her hair a thorough brushing, leaving it to flow over her shoulders, loose and casual.

She was to be the aggressor tonight. There was a heady power in that thought, one that made her blood rush like quicksilver through her veins. She had never done anything like this before, yet the images it conjured up were tempting. Could she do it? How did a woman become the aggressor? She giggled lightheadedly.

She didn't hesitate until she reached his door. Then suddenly, and for the first time, she began to hear the voice of reason. What in heaven's name was she doing? But her feelings were stronger than her reason and she reached for the knob and pushed open the door to a new world.

Josh lay on the bed, his hands beneath his head. He wore the bottoms to a pair of black silk pajamas, his hair-roughened chest exposed to her view. His eyes devoured her as she stood in the doorway, but he never moved a muscle. Slowly she approached him, reaching the edge of the bed and staring down at him. Still he didn't move; her courage rapidly faded.

"It isn't easy, is it?" He knew too much.

"How do I know you won't play me wrong? Reject any advances I might make?" Her voice sounded like a hoarse whisper. She didn't even know she had spoken her thoughts out loud.

"You don't."

"Then why should I put myself through this only to be rejected?"

"Men don't know either, Candra. It's hard to lay your wants and feelings on the line, knowing that the person you're with could say no." He smiled slowly. "Now you know what it's like to be the one to make the first move. It's not as easy as it looks."

Her purpose faltered for a moment. Then she took a deep breath and sat down slowly, her hand reaching out to touch one small hard nipple, then shift sensuously down his chest toward his navel. His breath hissed in his throat, but still he didn't move, his muscles taut with expectancy.

"You're so beautiful," she whispered, her hands learning the contours of his body. She leaned over, trailing kisses from his shoulder to his jawline, feeling the clean raspiness of his skin. Her hand followed the trail of hair down his chest toward the dark cord of his pajama bottoms. She pulled the knot, her eyes never leaving his face. A muscle in his jaw twitched, but she kept her eyes locked with his as she slid down the obstructive material.

The building tension was almost unbearable, but she refused to give in to the demands of her own body until she had some sign from him. He had to show her, trust her, love her enough to allow at least a part of those invisible barriers to fall. Her heart thumped in her throat, the fierce longing for him almost more than she could bear. She needed him, wanted him. Couldn't he see that?

As if he read her mind he answered her unspoken question. "More, Candra. I want more from you."

"How much?" Her hands continued to trail down his lean thighs, her eyes locked with his.

"All you can give," he murmured huskily.

Slowly, tentatively, she leaned forward and shaped her lips to his, then pulled back, only to do it again and again. She teased his lower lip, nibbling the firm shape of it until finally he could take no more. His hands came from behind his head to pull her closer, mold her more fully to his long length. He stroked her back through the silkiness of her gown; his hands were sure, firm, as they touched the softness of her thighs before coming around and up to cup her swelling breasts. A rush of heat flowed through her, making her almost dizzy with its effect.

Though he was still holding something of himself back, Candra could feel the tense pressure of him, as if he were on a short rein and wanting to break through. The feeling of power enveloped her. He wanted her, he needed her, and the proof was in his controlled touch and short breaths. She was suddenly brave, knowing he couldn't resist, and she continued to tease him, taunt him with small butterfly caresses until she thought he could stand no more. With lightning swiftness she moved away from him, to stand tall and proud next to the bed, her eyes as hungry for the sight of his long lean body as he was for her own soft form. With an infinite slowness Candra slipped the top of the peach-colored gown from her shoulders to rest on her hips. She watched him watching her, hunger glittering in his eyes.

"You're a tease."

"Yes. But only for you."

"And you do it so well."

"You're my teacher. You've teased me ever since I

came here. Now I want you where you have had me these past days." A small smile played on her lips. With a swift and final movement the pleated gown slipped off her hips to slide caressingly down her long legs and settle on the carpet. She stood naked before him; slowly he took her in from head to foot.

"Do you like what you see?" she teased throatily, but behind her question was a thread of fear that he would find some flaw.

"I like," he growled. "Come here. Now."

And she did. Quickly he shifted his body over hers, the heavy weight of him pressing her into the contours of the bed. The feel of him above her was good, warm, right.

"I should have known you'd be like this." He ran a path of kisses down her throat to one budding nipple, teasing her now as she had done to him.

Her hands ran through his hair before grasping his shoulders as heat poured through her veins. "What did you expect?" she breathed into his ear.

"I hoped . . . this."

"And what is . . . this?"

"A woman who knows her own sensuality and isn't afraid of showing it, even when the chance of being refused is there. A woman who can give as much as she can take. You." His last word was muffled against her breast as his mouth sought all the small secret places that tuned her nerves to their highest pitch. But now there was no rush for him. He had what he wanted and they would both enjoy it to the fullest.

"Wait, sweetheart. It will get even better," he

whispered into the small hollow of her neck. "Wait." And she tried, but her feelings were swamping her reason. She clung to his shoulders as he took her to the peak of fulfillment, only crying his name aloud when she could stand no more.

His shaking hand swept back the dampened hair from her face, his eyes filled with tenderness and . . . was it love? She wanted his answer, needed to know just what she meant in his life, but as she began to form the question he kissed her, silencing the words.

"We'll talk later, darling. Right now I want you in my arms so I can sleep, knowing you can't disappear on me."

"What makes you think I'd try to go anywhere?" she asked, realizing for the first time just how tired she was. She snuggled closer to his body, her legs intimately entwining with his.

"I don't know. I just don't want to take the chance," he murmured sleepily, moving his arm so he could reach up and clasp one breast. He gave a deep sigh of satisfaction and together they slid into sleep.

Bright sunshine filtered through Candra's lids. Josh was leaning over her, a grin on his face and a cup of coffee in his hand.

"Wake up, sleepyhead. It's dawn and you're missing a spectacular scene put on by Mother Nature herself." He tilted the coffee cup to her waiting lips, kissing her quickly as he withdrew the cup. His eyes looked as if he wanted to tell her something, but then the gaiety was back and he turned, shutting out all communication except surface talk. "I'll give you fifteen minutes to get dressed and then I'll come barging in after you."

"To help me?" she teased, attempting to shrug off a feeling of doom. He hadn't said he loved her. Not last night and not this morning.

"To spank you for being slow." Then he was out the door.

She showered and dried quickly; then, wrapped in Josh's velour bathrobe, she skipped up the stairs and into her room. Dressing took only moments. She was eager to return to Josh's side and ask him all the questions that were poised on the tip of her tongue. Any answer would be better than no answer at all—she hoped.

The day was magic. She and Josh took a long walk by the banks of the Rogue River, hand in hand. There were so many other simple things that they didn't know about each other, so many small questions to be asked and answered. But occasionally there was a silence between them as deep and as still as the river itself. Despite her earlier eagerness, Candra couldn't bring herself to ask him to define his feelings for her. Last night had taught her a lot, but she was still deathly afraid of rejection. She would wait and bide her time. Soon, she told herself, he would explain everything to her and they could live happily ever after.

Dinner was over and Roddy was in bed before Candra's doubts began to push themselves to the forefront again. She tried to hide them in the back of her brain, but it wasn't working. She had to have a few answers.

As she came down the stairs Josh was staring up at her, a fresh cup of hot coffee in his hand. His eyes slid over her slim body and a warmth suddenly circulated through her, settling to rest in the pit of her stomach. Surely no man could look at a woman that way and not be in love with her.

Suddenly someone began knocking on the door, destroying the intensity of the moment. They both turned, startled when it was suddenly thrown open. From Candra's height she could see two people entering, one wrapped in furs from her blond head to her feet.

"Josh, darling!"

Josh walked quickly toward the door, but Pepe was faster, closing it silently as the company stood in the entrance of the living room.

Candra took a step up, staying in the shadows as she realized who the beautiful blonde was. Joan Macy stood as if poised on the stage, her arms outflung to expose the breathtaking flame-colored chantung dress beneath her full-length fur coat. Joan, the invisible woman on the telephone, the woman who had sung the songs on the tape. Josh's mistress.

Pain squeezed the blood from Candra's heart as she watched Josh go into the other woman's arms, giving her a warm hug and kiss on the cheek. She reciprocated, branding him with her blood-red lipstick. He made a step back, but he wasn't to be let off so lightly, for she cupped his chin with her slim, beringed hands and brought his mouth to hers in a searing kiss. Candra's eyes were glued to him, mesmerized by the sensuous scene below, her heart slowly breaking as she watched the intimate meeting.

Suddenly a man stepped from out of the shadows. He, too, was wearing a heavy coat, not fur, but what looked like expensive cashmere. "This weather is so unpredictable!" he growled loudly. "Why Joan had to see you now, when you were due to come down to Los Angeles in three days, is beyond me!" He pulled off his coat and handed it to the waiting Pepe. "But Joan wouldn't take no for an answer. You've really got some determined woman there," the man teased and a band tightened around Candra's heart, squeezing the breath from her lungs.

Josh laughed, a husky sound that filled the room. Could Candra detect a hint of strain in it? She didn't know. "You're with her more than I am, Bob," he said. "But what are you both doing here?" He looked down at the lovely Joan, who had hooked her arm possessively through his. "When I talked to you, you were busy with a recording session. Did you finish?"

Joan's throaty chuckle was like a knife in Candra's heart. "Darling, you acted as if you wanted me to stay away. And there's nothing like pushing me away to get my attention," she murmured coyly. "You aren't disappointed, are you? You were angry with me last month when I said I couldn't accompany you, so I'm here now . . . ready to make it up to you." Her hand rested on his shoulder, coaxing him to respond. "Aren't you glad to see me?"

The bile rose in Candra's throat and she fled to the sanctuary of her room, ignoring Josh's command to come back.

What a fool she had been! Her almost hysterical laugh turned into a cry as she leaned against the dresser, her trembling legs almost unable to hold her up. How could she possibly have thought that he was interested in someone as naive, inept and inexperienced as she was when Joan Macy was waiting in the wings? Another sob lodged in her throat, but she refused to let the tears fall. Shoulders slumped, she dragged herself over to the window; she was staring out at the glistening landscape, but seeing instead the beautiful Joan expertly kissing Josh.

She didn't hear the bedroom door open, but she knew almost immediately that someone was in the room. When she turned she saw Josh, standing just inside the closed door, his face a mask of concern. Candra stared at him as if seeing him for the first time and her heart turned over again. He was so handsome, so virile, the perfect foil for Joan's petite blondness. What was he doing here when Joan had more than enough to offer him?

Her chin tilted; she was determined not to allow him to know just how heartbreakingly painful the scene had been for her. Please go soon, her heart cried; I can't keep up this pretense forever.

"Why didn't you come downstairs?" His voice was low and husky. Was he afraid of being overheard?

"You seemed to be . . . otherwise occupied. I'm

just a guest in your home and I didn't see any reason to intrude."

"You're not a guest, dammit!" He ran an agitated hand through his hair in a gesture of impatience. His eyes were silently begging her to understand, but she knew that she had to ignore his signals or her pain would be even greater.

"What am I then? A potential mistress? A friend who's just passing through? A 'good friend'?" She spoke bitterly and her anger at the scene she had witnessed below came through in her words.

Josh took a step forward, but her upraised hand warded him off. "I thought I'd have more time," he muttered and she stared at him, willing him to continue and make sense out of her jumbled emotions. "It's not what you think, Candra."

"Really?"

His hands clamped down on her shoulders before she could turn away. "This will all work out, Candra. Trust me."

Candra nodded wearily, as if understanding, without understanding at all. Her thoughts were in a maelstrom and she was too numbed by her tumbling emotions to do more than agree.

"Are you coming to my room tonight?" he asked softly, one hand tilting her chin so he could see the light in her eyes. "Or have you been scared off?"

Her face registered her disbelief. "You mean you still want me to, to . . ." She shook her head as if to clear it. "Your mistress is here now, so why do you need me?" She searched his face, hoping for a denial of the other woman's status, but instead a slow flush worked its way up his corded neck, confirming her doubts and turning them into a harsh reality.

"She has nothing to do with you and me, or our relationship," he growled roughly before his lips lowered in a bruising kiss that completely swamped all feelings except one—the desire to be possessed by him. He tore his lips away as a voice echoed through the door.

"Darling, where are you? What a shabby way to treat your guests!" The other woman's laughter trilled through the air, along with a deep chuckle from the other man.

"If I were you, Joan, I'd make sure he paid for this inhospitable treatment!" the older man teased, once again joining in her laughter as they opened the door to Candra's room. An awkward silence filled the air for a moment and Joan's eyes narrowed on Candra. She had obviously summed up the scene quickly.

"Darling, is this your new secretary?" the blond woman purred as she walked over to stand next to Josh, once more hooking her arm possessively with his. "Aren't you going to introduce us?"

Josh continued to stare at Candra as if he hadn't heard the question.

"Bad manners seem to be your forte lately," Joan said sweetly, giving him a coy look through her lashes, "so I'll introduce myself. I'm Joan Macy, Josh's fiancée."

Candra's face turned white and she reached for the dresser to keep her balance as the room began to spin crazily. Finally, her eyes accusing, she turned to

Josh, begging him to disagree, yet knowing the words were true. His own angry face confirmed her worst fears. It was true. It was true.

"Go on downstairs, Joan. I'll join you later," Josh said quietly, but his voice brooked no argument. The woman unwound her arm from his and quietly stepped outside, taking her astonished friend with her.

Candra's legs gave way and she found herself being held up by Josh's strong arms. She fought him then, hitting at him in silence. He took her blows quietly, without deflecting a single one. His face mirrored her own despair and she hated him all the more for it. Her arms were tired, but still she didn't stop until finally, totally exhausted, she crumbled in defeat. Her sobs sounded like gasps for air, but she couldn't seem to control them. Slowly, gently, Josh folded her against his chest, his hand soothing her back and giving her comfort the only way he could. She accepted it blindly, curling against him like a kitten looking for a warm home. Then she realized just where she was and pulled away, stiffening her arms to keep the distance between them.

"The world is full of surprises, Josh. But the biggest surprise of all is your engagement," she said hoarsely, holding onto her last vestige of pride. "You should have told me sooner. I would have brought you a present. Maybe a cruise for two up the Rogue River."

"Candra, let me . . ." he pleaded, only to be interrupted by her slightly hysterical laughter.

"You certainly knew what you were doing, Josh.

Stringing me along at this particular time in my life was just sheer genius. I doubt if any other time would have been as good! But now your fun in punishing me for all my past sins is over." Her voice disappeared in a sob, but she pulled herself together to continue. "And thank you for confirming all my doubts concerning your integrity."

"Candra, you don't understand and you're too upset to listen to me now. I'll discuss my 'integrity' with you in the morning." His gaze took in her ravaged appearance and once more his eyes softened with regret. "Tomorrow morning, after I've made love to you all night and I can hold you in my arms, exhausted, and know you have no choice but to listen to reason."

"Whose reason, Josh? Yours or mine?" Candra turned and walked toward the window before facing him again. Her eyes glistened with tears at the betrayal and hurt she felt. "I want you to know that I never want to see you again. Ever. Now get out of here. Go!"

The door closed silently and, like a flower in a windstorm, Candra sank to the floor, her head resting heavily on her knees. In a moment she would get up and go downstairs. Josh would laugh in that husky way of his and tell her it was all a joke, that none of this had really happened. But it had, and the facts couldn't be changed.

How odd to think back to that first night that seemed a century ago and remember that she had thought then that he wanted his revenge. Josh had chosen the perfect way to strike back at her. Lull her into a state where she wanted nothing but to be with him, regardless of her own morals and emotional makeup, then punch her in the stomach with the fact that it had been a setup. It was perfect.

A dry racking sob escaped her throat, but tears didn't follow. *She would not break down again!*

Candra pulled herself up from the floor and forced herself to settle down at the window seat, knowing she wouldn't be able to sleep any time soon. Occasionally laughter from downstairs intruded on her thoughts, but she did all she could to ignore it.

Much later Candra heard footsteps along the hall, telling her that the guests were going to bed. There were whispered words, then silence. Had Josh kissed Joan good night? Had he held her voluptuous form to his and felt the softness of her? Candra couldn't think about it. A chill ran down her body and she moved to change into a nightgown and a long robe, both of a pale blue color that accented the brightness of her eyes. But she wasn't going to Josh's room. That decision had been made earlier and she wouldn't revoke it. No matter how much her body cried out for release from the tension that the very thought of him aroused, her intellect told her she was a lucky woman to have found out early that being wanted wasn't the same thing as being loved.

Once more she sat on the window seat and stared out at the darkened landscape. The two rooms next to hers still had their lights on, the rectangles of light showing clearly on the hillside directly behind the house. One light was doused, then, finally, the second. Only then did she realize that Josh's light was still on. She could see his clearly defined shadow as he stood in front of the window. She became a trembling mass of nerves when she realized that he could also see her. His hand came up to wave and she quickly pulled away from the window, walking to the center of the room. She clenched her hands together to keep from opening her door. She would not go to him.

A small moan came from Roddy's room and she walked through to him, entering quietly so as not to waken him. He was much warmer now; he obviously had a fever. She always carried children's aspirin in her purse, so she quickly got some and woke him briefly to take the medicine. He settled back down to sleep almost immediately. She kissed his forehead lightly and frowned. She had given him the last of the pills and the thought that he might wake later, when she had nothing to give him, bothered her. She knew that she could always use a partial adult-strength aspirin, and she had seen a bottle of those in the kitchen. She decided to go down for a supply.

Quietly she picked her way down the darkened stairs toward the kitchen. The small light above the counter was on, a night-light for anyone who might need it. Her eyes quickly accustomed themselves to the dimness and she found the cabinet she needed, locating the aspirins within seconds. She was opening the bottle when she heard the distinct tapping of heels. Peering over the bar area, Candra had a full view of the living room and stairs—and the beautiful Joan who trailed down as if she was a movie starlet in front of the camera. Her pale pink peignoir billowed out around her, outlining her figure to perfection. She left the staircase, then walked quickly and decisively toward the back hallway and Josh's room.

Candra hardly even realized that she was following the woman. Joan knocked quickly, rapping lightly on the heavy wood. Candra stood several feet behind her, just inside the shadows so Josh wouldn't see her. The door opened, silhouetting Josh, who was naked except for his pair of black silk pajama bottoms, against the light.

"Darling, are you surprised?" Joan teased huskily, her voice crashing against Candra's ears. "I know you told me we would talk in the morning, but I can't wait until then. Let's talk now." Her voice held a smile. "Or something." Her arms locked around his neck, drawing his lips down to hers. She gave him a light kiss before her lips traveled across the mat of hair on his chest, little feline noises echoing in her throat.

It wasn't until Josh shifted his hand to cradle her blond hair that Candra finally moved into action. But she wasn't careful enough, for Josh noticed the movement in the shadows and looked up to see Candra in the instant before she turned away, her face a complete void. Only her bright blue eyes showed the agony of her soul as it was slowly ripped apart by the scene in front of her. She walked quickly away, stopping only when she reached the privacy of her room. She flicked out the overhead light and leaned against the door in the cool darkness.

And she thought she had put her emotions in the deep-freeze. Whatever she had felt when she had seen Josh and Bettina together all those years ago was now multiplied by a thousand. She had never known such hideous pain as that which seared through her veins to scorch her very soul now. It hurt so badly that she could hardly catch her breath. She allowed her racking sobs the freedom they demanded, hoping they would quench the searing fire.

The banging on the door reverberated through her body, scaring her into silence.

"Candra! Open this door!" Josh ordered.

Her voice was barely above a whisper as she gave him her answer. "Go away! Leave me alone!"

"I want to talk to you! Now!"

"No."

"Honestly, Josh! It's not the end of the world!" Joan's voice came clearly through the door. "I don't know why you're so upset, darling. She only works for you; she's not your future mother-in-law, for goodness' sake!" she continued. "She should have kept to her room if her sensibilities were so easily shocked."

Josh must have turned toward the singer, for his voice was almost too muffled to make out. "Just go to bed, Joan. We'll discuss this in the morning," he grated, then Candra heard his footsteps receding down the hall and toward the stairs, leaving Candra and Joan with just the door between them.

"I just don't understand," Joan muttered. Finally the click of heeled slippers told Candra that Joan had decided not to confront her tonight.

Candra paced the floor, her bare feet cool against the highly polished floor. Once in a while she would stare out her window to see the square of light still blazing from Josh's room below. But it gave her no comfort to know that he, too, was still awake. Instead she felt as if she were the prey and he was the hungry lion.

It was four o'clock in the morning when Candra finally dropped off to sleep, but the first rays of dawn found her awake again. She had emptied herself of all feeling, and the packing was done for both her and Roddy. She felt as if she was once again a robot, with the real Candra standing two worlds away, watching this Candra's actions without emotion. She was safe from harm.

When she checked Roddy he still had a low grade fever, but his breathing was even. With a small sigh of relief Candra slipped into a pair of jeans and a velour pullover and went quietly down to the kitchen. With a little luck she would be able to get Roddy something to eat and be on the road before anyone else was up.

She glanced around the kitchen, loving the coziness of it. Strange how she had fit into this house so easily. But she should have known better than to hope for the moon. Happiness wasn't something that was dropped into people's laps. Not hers, anyway.

Candra concentrated on one step at a time, making orange juice and getting out the eggs.

"You couldn't sleep either."

Candra jumped. She hadn't heard anyone. She couldn't face Josh, she just couldn't.

"I slept well enough to rise early," she lied, reaching for the refrigerator door.

"The hell you did," he retorted softly. "You paced the floor half the night. I ought to know, I paced right under you."

"Oh? Conscience bothering you?" she queried, keeping her hands as busy as she could, hoping he wouldn't notice how they trembled.

8

—◆◆◆◆◆◆◆◆◆◆◆—

Are you going to listen to me, or just pretend to cook to keep from talking?" he asked impatiently, running a hand around his neck as if to loosen taut muscles.

"I think last night said it all, don't you? I was set up for that little scene, wasn't I, just so you could taste revenge?" Candra turned to face him then and all the pent-up frustration and anger shone from her eyes. "Tell me, Josh, didn't it remind you of that scene in the barn all those years ago? What did you expect me to do this time? Tell Pepe? Am I still supposed to be that thirteen-year-old who clung so tightly to you that she didn't even allow you breathing space?" She gave a disgusted sound. "Well, I grew up, even if you didn't. I don't give a damn about your personal life and I'm certainly not hurt by it. It's none of my business what you do at any time. I don't know the reason behind your 'object lesson,' but I do know that I don't want a repeat performance. So if you would be kind enough to give me the keys to my car, Roddy and I will leave directly after breakfast."

"And go where?"

"To my uncle's house. This was to be a trial, remember? Well, my trial is over and I'm moving on. I won't interfere with your life this time, Josh. I don't think you're worth it."

"Still the same spoiled brat. You're still cashing in your marbles when the game doesn't go your way."

"Is that what you think this is? A game?" She laughed harshly. "I should have known."

They had both been so caught up in their argument that they hadn't realized that Joan was standing at the bar until she spoke. "Darling, whatever did you do to incur your little secretary's wrath so?" she purred as she walked around to stand next to Josh, her hand resting possessively on his arm.

Joan's laugh didn't seem strained, but the lines around her mouth told their own story. "Really, darling, you must be nicer to your employees. The poor girl looks as if she's frightened to death of you."

Josh's eyes continued to hold Candra's. Neither said anything as the silence became brittle. Finally Joan gave a small tug on Josh's arm to gain his attention. "Come on, darling. Why don't you introduce us?"

"Joan, Candra Bishop. Candra, my . . . fiancée,

Joan Macy," he said woodenly and Candra searched his face for a flash of emotion. There was none.

"Candra? My, aren't we informal!" The other woman came forward, her exotic gown of the night before still gracing her body. But her makeup was flawless, as was the long hair cascading down her back. "What were you doing last night, Candra?" Joan's eyes narrowed as she looked away from Josh toward Candra.

"I was getting aspirin for my brother." She waved a hand over the side counter, where the open bottle still sat. "And what were you doing? Or is that obvious?" Her voice was filled with contempt. Pain was still predominant, but another emotion was quickly making itself known—anger!

"It's obviously none of your business," the other woman snapped.

"You're right. It is none of my business. And now, if you'll excuse me, I have to feed Roddy and double-check my packing."

"Packing?" Joan questioned. "Does that mean you're leaving?" Her good nature had obviously been restored by that piece of news.

"She's not going anywhere. She's staying right here," Josh gritted, looking at her for the first time, his temper barely under control.

Candra slammed down the frying pan, her tensed nerves snapping. "I am *not* staying! I'm leaving today!"

"The devil you are!" Josh shouted, apparently forgetting the fact that Joan was still there, her mouth opened in amazement as she took in every word.

"You can't tell me what I can and cannot do, Josh. Not anymore! Why don't you take care of your own 'affairs' and keep your nose out of mine!"

His anger was almost overpowering as they glared at each other across the room. Josh took a step toward her and she felt chills along her spine as she retreated, fear making her eyes dilate.

"Candi!" Roddy's voice broke the spell. Candra's eyes moved toward the balcony, seeing even from that distance that Roddy's face was flushed with fever. He stood in his pajamas, his hands clenching and unclenching on the railing as he pleaded for help.

Within seconds she was up the stairs and scooping him into her arms. She walked him back to his bedroom, glancing over her shoulder when she reached the door to see Josh ushering Joan into the hallway and presumably into his bedroom.

Roddy was ill. His cold was twice as bad as earlier and now his stomach was upset, too. She replaced his sweat-soaked pajamas with a fresh pair, then shooed him back into bed. She gathered the laundry and left, promising to be back with aspirin right away.

Her numbed mind told her to do the next thing, then she could leave. Do the laundry and then she could leave. Get Roddy's fever down and then she could leave. She marched down the stairs with a purposeful step, ignoring the blanket of agony that seemed to cover her heart.

She got Roddy his aspirin, then went to wash his laundry. As she stood near the machine she could hear voices raised in anger. At first she thought they were coming from Josh's bedroom, then realized they were in the study.

"You told me you have a secretary and a child living here and allowed me to assume she's an older woman! What am I supposed to think? I've always been level with you, Josh. Couldn't you have given me some warning? If you wanted to break our engagement all you had to do was ask me."

"Enough, Joan," he interrupted.

"It's not enough! I have a few things to say and I'm going to say them. I want to know exactly what's going on and why! Give me some answers! You're supposed to belong to me."

"I don't belong to anyone, Joan. Not even you."

"We're supposed to get married next month and you tell me this *now?*" Her voice rose even higher. "I think it's time we discuss this. Let's get this settled now, Josh."

Candra's hands were shaking, her legs barely holding her up, and she leaned against the washer. Her stomach churned with tension as she absorbed the other woman's words. It was impossible to stop listening to the voices on the other side of the door unless she left, so she did, almost running in her haste to reach the stairs.

Her head was bent and she wasn't watching where she was going, so she ended up running headlong into the man who had come with Joan last night. He was wearing a pair of blue silk pajamas with a matching robe. Didn't anyone dress around here?

Pulling herself together, Candra stepped back

from his chest. "I'm sorry," she murmured, holding on to his arms for balance. She needed someone else's strength right now. She could hardly hold herself up after the scene she had just overheard.

"I'm not." The man called Bob chuckled. "So you're the new . . . uh . . . secretary we've come to investigate." He nodded knowingly at her bewildered look. "Oh, yes. Joan wouldn't let Josh out of her sight if she thought there might be a chance that someone else would snap him up. She's possessive, our Joan."

"How nice. Are you both engaged to her?" An amazed look crossed the older man's face before he burst out laughing, but his eyes were narrowed and humorless.

"As far as I'm concerned you're both welcome to her!" She pulled away from his grasp, reaching toward the bannister for support. "She looks like some prize filly, but then, he's an excellent stablehand!" She turned toward the stairs, but from the corner of her eye she caught a movement. She turned slowly. Joan and Josh stood in the doorway.

"You must think you know him very well to intimate what he is and isn't," Joan said sweetly, her eyes belying the tone of her voice.

"Ask him," Candra retorted. "He's yours—if you can hold on to him long enough."

The air was taut with strain as Joan sucked in her breath, her eyes shooting sparks of anger as she looked from Candra to Josh.

"For someone who came into this house with so

much civilized control, you've reverted to savagery very well," Josh sneered, his voice cold.

"I'm a fast learner, especially when an 'expert' is willing to teach me." Candra turned and walked up the stairs.

"Candra! Come back here!" Josh bellowed, but she ignored him, concentrating on taking one step at a time, her mind consumed with the thought of not collapsing until she reached her room.

"What the . . . ?" Bob stood in the center of chaos, his expression one of total noncomprehension.

"Shut up!" Josh growled. Just as Candra made it to her door she heard Josh's footsteps, then the slam of the front door.

An hour later Candra walked through the bathroom and into Roddy's room. His forehead was still burning with fever. She had never felt so frustrated before. There was no way she could bundle the small boy up and get them both out of here until he was better.

When she gave him more aspirin she felt his forehead; his dry skin was hot to the touch. She gently washed him down with a cool washcloth to keep the fever from climbing any higher. Her forehead was wrinkled with worry when the door opened and Josh stalked in, stopping only when he reached the bed and placed a hand on the small boy's head.

"He needs a doctor." He sounded concerned, all his anger gone. He gave Roddy a smile that brought an answering grin. "I'll call one immediately."

"That won't be necessary. Just give me his address and I'll take Roddy to him."

"Cut it out, Candra, and do what I tell you. You're going to put aside your little spoiled rich girl act and play the part you've undertaken. You'll take care of Roddy properly. He comes first. Do you understand?"

"Go back to your fiancée and leave me to my own business!" Candra came to her feet in agitation, humiliation and anger glowing in her eyes.

"You're staying until Roddy is well enough to travel," he went on, ignoring her. "Perhaps by that time I'll have this mess straightened out."

"Oh? And I suppose I'm just supposed to hang around here pretending I work for you so you have someone to make passes at while your bride-to-be arranges her wedding?" she retorted bitterly.

He gave her a look of disgust as he turned and walked toward the door. "I'm calling the doctor and you're going to stay here and take care of Roddy properly." His eyes bored into hers, softening as he saw her trembling chin. "Oh, Candra, don't jump to conclusions and head off in the wrong direction. You might find that where you want to go is where you just came from." The door closed too quickly for her to respond, even if she could have thought of anything to say. Frustration welled inside her.

Roddy sat up in the bed, his widened eyes giving away his feelings more than any words could. She soothed him and tried, stumblingly, to give him some sort of explanation. Then she smiled at him reassuringly, giving him a quick hug and promising to hold his hand until he fell asleep.

When Josh had held her in his arms, she had felt as if she was at the end of a very long and arduous journey, as if she had found her way home.

Josh was the only reward her heart wanted. He was everything and she loved him with all her soul. And he was someone else's.

Roddy moaned and Candra reached forward to feel his head. He was still too warm. A few minutes later Bob stuck his head in the room and told her that the doctor would be there later. Candra nodded, all her energies once more focused on the small body in the bed. When Roddy finally fell asleep Candra stood, pressing her hands against the small of her back and rubbing the tensed muscles. She had been bending over him for over two hours. That, plus the strain of the morning, had taken its toll. She was exhausted.

The door opened and Josh stood in the doorway, his eyes running over her slim form, showing his concern. "He's asleep?" he questioned softly and Candra nodded.

She didn't notice the tray in his hand until he moved to put it on the dresser. "I don't know how good it is, but anything is better than an empty stomach." Candra could have argued with him, especially after catching a glimpse of burnt toast, but it would have been too much effort.

For the first time Candra heard pots and pans clanging and rattling. "Pepe?" she questioned, glancing at the small dab of strawberry jam with crumbs sticking to its surface.

"Joan." Josh moved toward the window, his broad shoulders outlined against the sun. "Not the best cook in the world, not even in a pinch."

Candra didn't think before she spoke. "Her talents must lie elsewhere." The picture of the two of them the night before danced in her mind, tormenting her with emotions better left buried.

"Apparently." Josh was distant again. He picked up the coffee and handed it to her. "Drink up. It's probably the only edible thing on the tray."

Candra sipped quietly, hoping he would go away before she broke down and cried for all the lost things in life. Love. Second chances. People. Everything.

"Candra?" His fingers slid up her neck to raise her chin so he could stare deeply into her eyes. "Are you willing to listen to an explanation now?" His voice was quiet, but not to be ignored.

Her shoulders slumped. She was too exhausted to argue. Candra nodded, finally admitting to herself that she wanted to hear what he had to say more than anything, even if he was going to tell her to go away and never see him again.

"I know it was a shock for you to hear about Joan. I was going to explain the situation to you, but the time passed so quickly, and before I had a chance she walked in the door." He grimaced slightly, making her give him a watery smile. "I wasn't trying to pay you back in kind. You know that, don't you?"

She nodded, loving the feel of his hand against her

skin. "I know. And I even think I understand. But will your girl friend? If I were her I certainly wouldn't trust you. Not enough to marry you." Her jibe must have hit home with a vengeance. Josh's face turned white; then he drew himself up, knotting his jaw. Why shouldn't she hurt him as much as he had hurt her? She stood her ground, lifting her chin determinedly and edging away from the touch of his hand. "I think we've both suffered enough for what happened all those years ago. The best thing we can do for each other is to lead separate lives. I don't want to hurt you or Joan, and I'm certainly not masochistic enough to want to be hurt."

"And could I hurt you, little Candra?" His eyes gleamed with hidden light.

Candra looked away, her face drawn with strain. "Yes," she finally admitted. "And I don't think I could handle it very well. I have enough guilt feelings where you're concerned."

"What kind of guilt feelings?" Joan stood at the door, her hands clenching the knob as if she would break it off. "And why do I keep finding you two together every time I turn around? What is going on?"

"Go downstairs, Joan. We'll talk later." Josh sounded harsh and bitter, dismissing her as if she meant nothing.

"I want to discuss this now! If there are any plans that are changing, don't let me be the last to know. I won't be made a laughingstock!" Joan exclaimed heatedly, calming slightly only when Candra motioned to her brother, asleep across the room. "You never even noticed that there were women in the world until I came along. You thought none of us was worthy of you! Then I sang your songs and they become hits!''

Candra's head reeled, her face turning white. She turned haunted eyes toward Josh. ''You're Joshua Scott, the songwriter?'' she whispered. Her eyes mirrored the hurt she felt so deeply. He had kept this intimate piece of news to himself, too. ''I should have known, but it never really registered.'' She made a mock curtsy, tears beginning to fill her eyes in contrast to her overbright smile. ''Congratulations. I had no idea I was working for the great Joshua Scott! I certainly play the fool admirably for you, don't I? What a laugh I must have been. I'm only sorry my father isn't here to see you. He was always telling me he might have misjudged you.'' Candra straightened up slowly, then walked to the door, where Joan stood watching the scene. ''And now, if you don't mind, I'd like permission to leave the room and get cleaned up. The doctor should be here soon. Besides, I'm sure you and your fiancée have a lot to discuss.''

''Candra!'' Josh took a step toward her, but she backed away, almost stumbling in her haste to retreat, tears still glistening in her eyes.

''That's all right. You don't have to explain anything to me. I'll be as generous with you as you've been with me. You can have my ashes and hair shirt as soon as I'm through with them.'' Josh glowered at her, taking another step, but she held out her hand to keep him away. ''Seeing as I've already done most of my penance on your behalf, you should be able to wear it soon. I think you could wear it for the next twenty years and it wouldn't be enough." By the time she made it to her own room and closed the door a wall of blankness surrounded her and she wanted to keep it there. She felt betrayed.

Candra still felt nothing as she returned to Roddy's room later, staring out the window at the scene below.

The doctor arrived by late afternoon, harried and out of sorts. "I'm afraid both his ears are infected," he told her. "He'll be on antibiotics for the next two weeks. Meanwhile, I want him kept in bed, well covered, and drinking plenty of fluids. Has he always been this thin?"

Candra nodded. "Yes, he burns everything off. Lately he seemed to be keeping his weight level, though."

"Just wait, he'll get strong in this climate." He ruffled Roddy's hair with a friendly grin. "You stay here much longer, buster, and you'll look like a lumberjack in no time!" Roddy's giggle sounded more like a rasp.

"I'm glad there's something to laugh about up here, because it's chaos downstairs." Joan stood in the doorway, her smart gray wool slacks and black cashmere sweater accenting her blond hair. Her lips pouted prettily, but her puzzled eyes were pinned on Candra. But Candra's composure was in place now, along with a coolness that would be hard to break through.

"The doctor has just assured me that Roddy will be completed recovered in two weeks."

"Does that mean you won't be leaving?" Joan asked, pulling no punches.

"It means I'll be here for another week if Josh agrees."

"Josh has never been inhospitable or a fool," the doctor said emphatically, his eyes glancing from Candra to Joan and back again.

"I doubt if any of us could say we've led exemplary lives, Jim," Joan drawled.

So they knew each other. How cozy. Everyone knew everyone, except Candra. Odd man out . . . again.

Joan broke into her thoughts. "Since you're going to be around for a while, how about taking over the kitchen? Pepe had to go to San Francisco, so now we need someone to take over the cooking."

"I wasn't hired as a cook, Miss Macy," Candra said quietly.

Joan's face fused with color. "I wasn't implying that you were. I'm not a good cook, but you looked like you were doing okay this morning. And I am fairly good with children." She shrugged, embarrassed. "I'm not quite as heartless as most people think. I could help take care of Roddy for you."

At Joan's remarks a small dart of pain got through Candra's armor. The thought of Joan and Josh and their children hurt deeply. She would have to keep her wall firmly in place.

"All right, Joan," she said resignedly. "Just give me a minute first." She turned to the doctor and stretched out her hand. "Thank you so much, Dr. Jefferson. You have a way with children and their worried guardians." She smiled her gratitude.

The doctor smiled warmly in return, clasping her hand longer than was necessary. "No trouble at all. I'll be back later in the week to see how he's doing. Meanwhile, if you need me just call my office." He turned to leave, his little black bag almost out the door before he was. "By the way, I should be back near here just about dinner time, if you'd care to invite me for a drink and a homecooked meal."

"I'd like to, but this is Josh's home. I'm only a guest," she reminded him gently.

"But with such esteemed company as yourself, Josh would certainly agree to entertain."

"What are you talking about, Jim?" Joan broke in curiously.

"I'm afraid that Portland society has a way of following people," Candra broke in. "Dr. Jefferson means that until two months ago I was a member of that illustrious society."

"Of course, I should have known! I remember the name now. You're Alicia Bishop's girl."

"No, Alicia was my stepmother, not my mother." Candra bowed her head, retreating from the memories.

Joan watched her closely as she mused. "I met her a few times in San Francisco, just after her husband died. I must say, she didn't seem a bit like you."

"She wasn't."

They got her point and both turned to leave, the doctor giving a few last minute instructions before he descended the stairs. Candra tucked Roddy back in, then walked downstairs and into the kitchen. It was five o'clock and dinner was supposed to be served around seven. She had to concentrate all her energies on fixing a decent meal. Everything else could be tackled later.

9

All Candra's attention was focused on preparing the meal when Bob strolled over, a drink in hand and a smile on his face. He was dressed in a sweat suit and looked as if he had just gone through a hard workout.

"You've got to be good to be chief-cook-and-bottle-washer around here. Josh's housekeeper has always taken first prize. Even Pepe bows to her culinary skills."

"I could be the worst right now and it wouldn't matter. Pepe is in San Francisco, so I'm told." She glanced up, brandishing a knife. "Unless you want to do the honors?" she teased, showing just a bit of her former self.

Both hands rose in the air, palms out. "Not me!

My forte is more along the lines of strong coffee the morning after. Anything else and I'm all thumbs.''

Candra chuckled at the expression of mock horror on his face.

"How did you meet Josh?" Bob asked presently and Candra once more became wary, but his face was a bland mask. Apparently it was just an idle question.

"Josh worked for my father when he was a teenager," she answered, dicing carrots with intense concentration. "And what about you? How did you meet him?"

"Joan brought him to see me, telling me she wanted to sing his songs." He bit his bottom lip in concentration, "You see, I'm Joan's public relations manager. Now I do the same for Josh, although he makes it almost totally impossible at times. He keeps such a low profile that I have to work hard to earn my percentage."

"I see," she murmured, still unable to look at him.

"They've been together for four years now and only this past year have I been able to get him to agree to any publicity on them as a couple. But, as I'm sure you realize, publicity makes the world go round, and also helps newspapers and magazines sell, not to mention records. And there's nothing like a hot romance for that extra boost. When they tie the knot it should raise sales a good twenty percent, maybe more, if we're lucky." His eyes narrowed as he took a sip of his drink and watched carefully to gauge the effect of his words. But Candra didn't look up and the conversation soon moved into other channels. Eventually he went off to join the others.

Fruit salad sprinkled with fresh coconut sat in the refrigerator. Potatoes and carrots were in their serving dishes, ready to be popped into the microwave during the final stage. Thin-sliced cucumbers tossed with sour cream and sprinkled with dill sat on the counter; a broccoli and cheese casserole was next to the potatoes and a thick pot roast, seasoned to a turn, was in the oven.

Candra wiped her hands on a towel as she surveyed the kitchen with satisfaction. Six-thirty and all was well.

She pulled out the cutlery and began setting the dining room table. Where were the others? she wondered. In Josh's den, probably. What would she be doing two weeks from now? Where would she be? Should she continue on to her uncle's house or should she return to Portland to try to make a life for herself and Roddy? Her brain hurt with all the thinking that had gone into bringing her to this point. Not only was she fighting memories, but she was also ignoring the future. Everything she faced these days was unknown and untried, and she was so tired. So tired.

Slowly she climbed the stairs. She chose a plum-colored halter dress that brought out the highlights in her hair, which she had twisted into a small knot that rested on the nape of her neck. It looked severe, but it suited her mood. Tonight her years of living with Alicia and her friends would hold her in good stead.

* * *

The early morning air was crisp and clear. The remaining snow crunched under Candra's boots as she dodged the trees to keep to the path along the high bank of the Rogue River. She had been up almost all night after dinner the night before. In the darkness of her room she had watched the moon travel across the sky. Everyone had gone to bed and the house was silent. Then footsteps softly padded along the hallway, stopping at the head of the stairs in hesitation, then making an almost silent trip down to the living room. The footsteps faded away, but Candra knew too well to whom they belonged and where they were going.

She had stared at the ceiling, tears streaming down her cheeks to dampen the pillow. Josh would be opening his door just about now, just as he had done before. The light from the room would darken his skin even more, turning it into a deep warm bronze. He would fold Joan in his arms, his lips on hers . . . She had turned over in bed and sobbed into her pillow. Why did love hurt so much?

Candra broke off a small limb from a dead tree and continued her early morning walk. The Rogue River. How appropriate it was for Josh to live on its banks. He was so roguish himself. One minute he held her in the security of his arms and couldn't let her go, the next he was holding someone else. He could be tender with her, wiping tears from her face, but then he could lash out with words that pierced her heart. But as often as she threatened to leave, she couldn't imagine being anywhere else, not so long as he still wanted her here.

The sound of a horse's hooves reached her and Candra was drawn from her reverie immediately, knowing who it was and not wanting to meet him. Josh sat so handsomely on his bay horse, his breath vaporizing in the cold morning air. He wore jeans and a brown turtleneck sweater that hugged his muscled arms. A tanned sheepskin-lined vest was zipped up over his broad chest and a western hat covered his dark hair. He tugged at the reins as he stopped just a foot or so away from her. She wanted to run, but she was caught between the river and a huge old tree, and she knew he wouldn't allow her to pass him. Better to stay and bluff her way through this encounter.

"Good morning. Where's Joan?" She was amazed that her voice sounded so calm, even to her own ears.

"I want to talk to you." His mouth tightened in anger.

"And I think that everything that needed to be said has been."

The tiredness in his eyes told her that he, too, had spent a restless night. Had he spent it all with Joan? A knife-edged pain twisted in the pit of her stomach.

"Are you going to listen?" His eyes searched hers for an answer. Was he silently pleading with her? "Somehow this entire thing has gotten out of hand."

Candra didn't trust herself to speak. Sticking her cold hands into her pockets, she stared at the twisted shadows of the trees as Josh dismounted to stand in front of her. He took her elbow and, with the bay trailing behind, guided her along the riverbank and toward the house.

"I knew someday I would see you again, Candra. If not for any other reason than to appease my curiosity. What I didn't know was *when* I would see you. Time passed quickly after I left Portland and I was busy with my career. But I thought of you often."

"Really? Why?"

He hesitated, taking her hand out of her jacket pocket to rest inside the warmth of his own. "In the beginning I hated you for lying about what you had seen. You told everyone I was making love to Bettina, but we hadn't gone anywhere near that far." He glanced at her for confirmation and she nodded reluctantly, knowing he was right. He had been holding Bettina close and kissing her, but no more.

"But mostly I hated your father for what he was making you become. He raised you with a minimum amount of care and understanding and every day that passed it showed more in your actions." They slowed to a stop and Josh faced her, bringing her chin up with his forefinger and lightly running his thumb across her lips to send heat through her veins. When he was satisfied with her reaction he turned and started walking once more, her hand still securely in his. "When you told your father you had seen me making love to Bettina in the barn you didn't know what a can of worms you opened." He stared straight ahead, his voice level. Candra continued to walk beside him, her head bent. There was no way to get away from this conversation. He had been determined from the beginning that they would have this discussion. All she could do was bear with it until it was over and then he would leave.

"Your father began remembering little incidents concerning us," Josh continued. "Like the time he found you wrapped around my waist in the barn. You had been crying because you couldn't go to New York with him as he had originally promised. When he saw us, I was comforting you. I was a boy of nineteen and you were like a little sister to me then."

Candra's startled eyes glanced up to the shadowed planes of his face. She didn't remember the incident. She had gone to him for comfort so many times. That her father, who had ignored her most of the time, would have remembered it amazed her.

"Because of the guilt your father felt toward you, he lashed out at me. He accused me of seducing you, too." At her gasp he gave her hand a squeeze, continuing, "Then, of course, everyone decided the best action was no action at all and no charges were ever filed. Bettina and her parents moved and I was booted out."

"I never knew. I never meant that to happen." Her voice was hoarse with the emotions that churned away inside. For the first time she fully realized what a messy chain of events had occurred because of her jealousy.

Once more Josh stopped, turning toward her. "I know that now. I knew that the first night you came here; it just took me a while to admit it. You were jealous and hurt, but you were never cruel. You're not that kind of person, Candra."

"How do you know?" Her eyes finally met his. A strange breathlessness was attacking her.

"The way you took care of Roddy, thanked Pepe for his help, did my letters with such dedication. At first the only thing I wanted from you was a bitter-sweet revenge. I lived with that thought for two or three years. Then one day I found myself *not* thinking of you and the way you had changed my life. I was building a new life, one that was infinitely better than before. I began remembering the good times we had together, the horses, the workers. I had a wonderful home in Portland for a few years, Candra." He smiled, taking the sting from his words, and she smiled slowly in return, warmth suffusing her veins at his intimate gaze.

"And you became a big success as a songwriter," she intervened.

"Not at first, but it came." He looked out at the swirling river as if his mind was a thousand miles away. Then he began walking again, the horse clip-clopping behind them. "My career really took off when Joan sang one of my songs, 'Little Girl with Golden Eyes.' She introduced me to Bob a little while later. He was her manager, one of the best in the business."

"You wrote that song?" She stared up at him. "That was one of my favorites! Why didn't I know?"

"No one ever remembers songwriters." He chuckled, giving her hand an intimate squeeze. "Unless they're publicized for doing something else. Which is how I became engaged to Joan."

"I see." He could feel her withdrawal and gave her hand a tug.

"No, you don't see! This is a lonely business, Candra. Everyone is out to get his share of the cake and not always with the best manners. I fought for my songs, recording, changing musicians and orchestration to fit with what we had to work with. Then I'd go home at night and sit in a lonely apartment and watch television while I ate a TV dinner because Pepe and I were too tired to cook something edible." He took a deep breath. "It was either that or go to another party with another set of faces that all looked the same."

"Oh, Josh," she murmured, her heart going out to him. She, too, knew what it was to be lonely. Her hand touched his chin, trying to soothe away the lines caused by lack of sleep and his confession. He clasped it and brought it to his mouth, caressing the palm with his lips.

"Let me finish, Candra," he muttered. "Then I'm going to kiss you breathless," he promised. "Joan and I were good friends. We worked well together as a team, the sound was just right. Finally we listened to Bob's suggestion and got engaged as a publicity stunt. It was Bob's idea, but he had no trouble getting us to go along with it. We were both lonely and tired of the party routine. Neither of us was involved with anyone else, so it seemed like a good thing to do. America loves sweethearts." His voice held a bitter note, but he brushed it aside with a small smile.

"Good old Bob." If Candra said any more she knew her voice would crack and give away the strength of her confused emotions. No wonder he had looked so angry, though, seeing all his plans go down the drain. Josh let go of her hand and clamped strong fingers to her slim shoulders, turning her roughly to face him.

"Don't act so damned understanding, Candra, when you really don't understand at all. I'll explain it over and over if I have to. You've got to understand for real!"

Instead of tears, anger came. How dare he assume that she was so dumb! She shook off his hands and took a step back, her blue eyes blazing. "You're right; I don't understand, but I don't see what difference that makes now! You're still engaged and that fact hasn't changed. And I already know what you think of me. You've made your position very clear. I'm the poor-little-rich-girl turned poor! Someone to console and make you feel as if you've done your good deed for the day! I'm another woman in your life, someone to add to your stable of female admirers. Someone to make love to when no one else is around!" She continued to storm, not caring that his green eyes were turning black with anger, his body stiffening.

"I'm tired of playing your games. You told me once that I tried to own people. Well, you may have been right, but you do a pretty good job yourself! Isn't owning someone shown by manipulating them?

Don't you manipulate me, Joan, Bob, even Roddy? You ask for a commitment from me, then you invite Joan into your bed!" Tears coursed down her cheeks and she swiped at them with one hand, streaking dirt across her cheek. "Well, I'm not buying it! I can't stand this seesawing back and forth. You like me, you hate me, you want me, you want Joan! You have a fiancée but you're 'just good friends'! Baloney!"

As suddenly as she had burst into flame, the fire burned out and Candra's face paled when she realized just how much of herself she had allowed him to see. Josh reached out and hesitantly she placed her hand in his again, her head bent down in supplication.

"You love me," he said quietly, his low voice rasping gently on her nerves. She was more aware of him than she was of the sun and moon, the air she breathed, but she couldn't tell him so. She couldn't look at him, couldn't bear to see the triumph in his eyes.

His hand held hers, tightening to force her answer. "Say it," he demanded. "For heaven's sake, say it!"

"No!"

His voice was rough with emotion. "Candra, don't do this. Do you love me?"

"Yes." Her voice was a soft whisper, almost carried away in the warming breeze.

He moaned, folding her in his arms to hold her as close as their heavy coats would permit. They tasted of each other, neither able to get enough of the honeyed sweetness of their loving. Waves of dizziness assailed her and she clung to the thickness of his vest, pulling him closer. She could feel the tautness of his thighs, and reveled in her discovery. Surely he must love her, surely he must! He pulled away, as obviously reluctant to leave her for the trip to L.A. as she was to have him leave.

"Look at me, Candra," he ordered, his fingertips moving along her slim neck to rest just under her chin. He tilted her face toward his and she could see the magical wonder mirrored in his eyes.

"I love you, Candra. I love you more than you'll ever know." His lips teased hers briefly, gently. "Let me get this nonsense in L.A. out of the way, then I'll be back and we can make our plans," he promised huskily.

"What about Joan?" Although it was plain that Josh didn't love the other woman, Candra knew deep down that Joan was truly in love with him. The funny thing was that Candra didn't think Josh knew of the singer's love.

"Joan came downstairs last night and we talked it out. The engagement is off. She knows I love you," he said firmly. "I didn't invite her to my room, Candra." He looked grim and she shuddered at the thought of his wrath. "I was so sure it was you that it took me a minute to realize she had taken the initiative."

"But why, Josh? I don't understand." Her heart was bursting with her love for him, but she still didn't understand his motives.

He frowned before answering. "I wasn't very sure

of you. I knew you cared for me, but I didn't know how much. I thought that I would know if I made you commit yourself first."

Laughing joyfully, Candra threw her arms around his neck. "You crazy nut! I've been committed to you for practically forever; I was just too afraid to let you know. Then, when I heard about your engagement, I was so confused all I wanted to do was run away and hide in a hole."

His laughter joined hers and it was the release of a lifetime for both of them. All they needed was each other. And they had that.

Later they walked the horse slowly toward the barn. A shadow crossed Candra's face.

"What's the matter, darling?" Josh asked, tenderly, stopping in the middle of the trail to hold her closely once more. "What's bothering you?"

Candra gave a deep sigh, her arms traveling around the bulky waist of his coat. "Poor Joan. I'm so glad for us, though."

"It couldn't have been any other way. Don't you know that?"

She listened to the even tempo of his heart, which beat in unison with hers. "Now I do," she said softly.

His lips lowered to hers and her heart leaped with the ecstasy of his touch. She clung to him as his tongue explored the softness of her parted mouth. Their clothes were too bulky to let her feel the warmth of his body and she groaned her frustration, wiggling closer to him. Josh pulled away, taking a ragged breath.

"What I can't feel my imagination is telling me is there. If you don't want to be made love to on the cold ground we'd better head back." His voice vibrated in her ears and his eyes were sending messages she was hard pressed not to respond to. His intensity frightened her almost as much as it delighted her. With a nod they turned and, arms around each other's waists, walked toward the barn.

An hour later he was gone, along with Joan and Bob. Candra stood at the window staring at the car tracks that led away from the house and down the dirt drive. He had promised he'd be back a week from today. He had promised . . .

10

Candra found it hard to keep her happiness bottled up inside. Even three days after Josh left for Los Angeles she was as buoyant as a child's helium balloon. She wanted to shout her love to the world. Then doubts would flood her and her spirits would sink. When he returned would he love her as much as she imagined? Or was his love a dream? Then, each night, he would call and she would be flying again.

Roddy was recovering fast; he was gaining weight and almost all his medicine was gone. He was allowed downstairs now and loved sitting on the couch in front of a roaring fire while Candra read to him from one of his favorite books. He wanted to get well soon so he'd be able to help Pepe with the animals again.

By the end of the third day Candra couldn't stand the inactivity anymore. After dinner she shooed Pepe out and cleaned the kitchen. Then, without realizing it, she began pacing back and forth in front of the fireplace, tense because of the weather, which had turned stormy again, and her own emotions.

Pepe silently handed her a glass of wine with a cinnamon stick for a swizzle.

"Thank you, Pepe. I must need some exercise. As soon as the weather warms up I'll do the shopping." Her voice was high and forced, rattling on and on. She was nervous and wished that Josh would call now to tell her again that he loved her. Was he working? Was he with Joan? Did they spend a lot of time together? There were so many questions without answers running around in her mind, but when Josh called they fled into the dark recesses of her thoughts, not to return until the call was over.

"Why don't you work off some of your energy in the gym?" Pepe broke into her thoughts, his quiet voice grabbing her attention. She turned to stare at him in surprise. "You would sleep better after the whirlpool."

"How do you know I'm not sleeping well?" Her skirt swished softly against her long legs as she continued to pace. Had he heard her walking the floor at night?

"I've seen the light on in your room."

"I'm sorry if I've disturbed you," she said stiffly, suddenly embarrassed. Did he also know how her arms ached to hold Josh? Did he realize that Candra craved Josh's kisses so much that she couldn't sleep as she waited for his return?

"You didn't disturb me. If you were gone and Josh were here he, too, would be awake."

"Thinking of new songs?"

"Thinking of you," Pepe stated dryly, as if she had fished for that information.

"I love him." It was so good to say it out loud!

Pepe smiled. "I know," he said softly, but with a wealth of feeling. He took her glass and headed for the kitchen. "If you want to get your robe I'll start up the whirlpool for you. It will help you rest."

Shortly after that Pepe stuck his head in the door and told her that everything was ready; then he left for his own apartment, which was attached to the barn.

She undressed in the quiet of the gym. Her jumbled thoughts screamed at her in the silence. As with every other room in the house, there was a small cassette player on one of the shelves, and she reached forward, placing a tape in the slot.

One of Josh's songs drifted through the air, and she sighed as she slowly edged her way into the warm whirlpool. The jets of warm, bubbly water eased her tension.

A sigh left her throat, turning into a moan of delicious pleasure as she sank deeper into the frothy water. A wisp of hair escaped her loose topknot and she tried to push it back in place, then froze as she watched the door open and a shaft of light beam through. Her shocked eyes locked with Josh's, deep blue ice melting under his warm green gaze. He entered, his smile telling her of his pleasure at seeing her there.

"Josh." Her mouth formed his name, forcing it through provocatively parted lips. It was an invitation, and he walked toward her, only to stop when he reached the edge of the small tub.

Her hands crossed over her breasts in a protective gesture. "When did you come back?" she asked breathlessly, unable to stop her heart from beating in double time.

"Apparently just in time," he answered, his eyes roaming over every part of her body, which was barely hidden under the softly bubbling water. He seemed to be endowed with X-ray vision, for his eyes grew darker than emeralds. She watched him unbutton his shirt with deliberate movements, mesmerized by the intangible intensity that hung in the air between them.

It took forever, it took a second, then he was in the water, his bronzed body glistening in the water that swirled around them, bringing them closer together until his lips reached hers. His arms encompassed her, bringing them as close as two people could be. The entire length of their bodies touched and parted and touched again to build such a longing inside her that she was sure he could see it in her eyes, When he had kissed her on the riverbank she had wanted this to happen. She had always wanted him. The memory of his embrace had kept her up at night, wandering through the darkened house.

"My God, I've missed you!" he groaned, one

hand slipping beneath the water to cup her breast, teasing it to a fullness meant just for him. "I love you, Candra."

"I love you," she whispered in return.

Her hand found his chin, rough with a day's growth of beard, etched his brows, stroked the planes of his face. One finger followed the strength of his jawline to rest lightly on his firm lips. This was the way it should be. This was what love should be like.

"I knew you'd be wonderful to know and hold." His hands held her tight. "After I left Portland I tried to reach you by phone once or twice, but you had been sent to boarding school. I found myself worrying about you."

"Boarding school was Alicia's idea. She thought I would stay out of trouble and out of her life," she whispered softly, her lips brushing teasing butterfly strokes across his.

"I saw you once, when you were sixteen or so. Pepe and I were passing through Portland. The car was parked in the driveway with the motor running, so I waited outside the gates. A few minutes later you came out and stood on the steps until your stepmother joined you." He nuzzled her neck, his whiskers lightly scratching her skin. She loved it. "You were dressed in a rust pantsuit and your hair hung down your back, straight and shining. But your face was the most interesting part of you. You were unhappy and it showed. I think I fell in love with you then. That's still the mental picture I carry around with me wherever I go."

His head was buried in her shoulder, smelling the

sweetness of her skin, their limbs entwining, bodies touching, molding, floating together in the warm water. When he raised his head his eyes glittered in the dim light, his gaze skimming the soft contours of her body. "You're as beautiful as I remembered."

"So are you," she responded huskily and he chuckled. It echoed in his chest and she could feel the vibrations. She arched against him, wanting to be closer, to dissolve inside him. His hands searched her, wandering from the fullness of her breasts to her ribs and down to her waist, stroking and stoking fires that would wait until he was ready for them to blaze. His hands traveled all over, creating rivers of flame wherever he touched.

"You're marrying me."

"Yes."

"Tomorrow."

"Yes."

"So docile," he teased, tugging gently on her earlobe with his teeth. Her breath caught in her throat and he captured her mouth with his in a kiss that was both passionate and possessive. Stars sprinkled across her closed eyelids as her bones turned to warm liquid honey. He made her respond to a simple touch as she had never done before. He teased her with an exquisite torture and her heart answered by heating her blood to a magical fever. He was deliberately taunting her, touching her until she cried out for fulfillment. His green eyes narrowed in satisfaction and he answered her pleas by crushing her body to his until her breasts strained against his massive chest. Her own hands were not idle, brushing his shoulders and back with sweet delight. Josh moaned as if in pain, grabbing her tighter in fierce possession before suddenly pushing her away.

"I should have waited outside," he muttered, staring at her stricken face. He reached out to tease her lips with his finger, his eyes tender with his love for her. "I want so badly to brand you as mine. I can hardly think straight when I'm around you."

Her forehead cleared in understanding and she blushed all over. He chuckled, his chuckles turning into laughter and she joined him. It waas a ridiculous situation and they both knew it!

"Joshua Scott Laurence, if you don't finish what you started I'll never forgive you," she said in mock anger, but her eyes told him just how much she needed his reassuring possession of her.

His eyes darkened with hidden passion that soon flamed into an inferno as he crushed her to his lean length, holding her as if he would never let her go. His tongue drew erotic patterns in her mouth, seeking, and in seeking giving such an intense pleasure that she moaned. He took her there, in the water, with all the passion and tenderness that she had ever hoped for, his knowlege of her superior to her own. He knew what she wanted and when she wanted it and where each touch would lead until she was begging for release. She cried his name and still he continued to torment her, until even he could take no more and claimed what she so freely offered. When their ecstasy blazed her breath caught in her throat, her eyes open wide to his own gaze as he watched the expression in her deep blue eyes. His lips came down to seal his possession, branding her fiercely with his kiss. They floated in the swirling water, arms wrapped around each other as the earth tilted slowly back on its axis.

His arms held her next to his lean, hard body, where she belonged. "You're adorable," he muttered, kissing the tip of her nose. "And shy, and lovely to look at, delightful to tease." He punctuated his list of her attributes with kisses on her lips, cheeks, eyelids. She loved it.

"Josh?"

"Hmmmm?" His mouth trailed fire across one full breast before pausing to nibble gently on the pebble-hard tip.

"What now?"

"We get married. Immediately." He sighed, running a hand through his dampened hair. "It's been hell down in L.A., filming that damned special. Especially knowing you were here."

"And everything was dandy for me, stuck here waiting for you?" She grinned.

"I hoped you were just slightly miserable. Misery loves company," he teased, then turned somber. "If you hadn't been here, I would have torn the state apart until I found you. Believe me when I say you'll never escape me, Candra. Your life is here, with me, in my arms from now on."

She nodded her understanding, knowing that their love was finally secure and would blossom for both of them. "Josh, will you mind caring for Roddy, too?" she questioned softly, still unsure of their new love and her place in his life.

"Roddy's a part of our family now. I can't imagine taking you without having him around to pester us." His voice was warm with humor, as if her fears were groundless.

"Positive?" she teased, suddenly exuberant.

"I'm positive, and you sound like an echo chamber." He chucked her lightly under the chin, then gave her a soft, swift kiss on the lips. "Come on, lady. I'll walk you to your door."

They dressed, then he turned off the tape and flipped the switch by the door, returning the room to darkness. They walked through the passageway slowly, hand in hand. Candra didn't want to let him go. Hadn't they just found each other?

Josh took her past the stairs and stopped just feet from his bedroom door, his hand tightening on hers to send shafts of heat through her veins. Sparkling green diamonds looked down on her, his gaze heating her excitement once more. They could hear each other breathing as they stood on the threshold of his room.

"Come here," he ordered huskily. "I want you in here."

Candra was led, unresistingly into his room. The darkness was broken by the full moon shining across his bed to light it as if it was an altar of love. But her love of him needed no proof. She felt ready to burst with the wonder of it and it shone from her eyes.

His trembling hands ran over her slim form to stop and mold her firm breasts. "You're everything I ever thought you'd be . . . and more," he murmured into her hair and her own limbs trembled with reaction.

He bent to scoop her into his arms, then laid her tenderly on the massive moon-drenched bed. The softness of the silk counterpane sent a quiver through her body; then Josh was there, holding her body next to his, warming her with his arms.

"Stay with me always, Candra," he whispered. "Stay in my arms for the rest of our lives. I'll never get enough of you. I don't want to be parted from you ever, even this night."

She snuggled close to him, loving the steady beat of his heart.

The words to his song returned to hum in her brain. Yesterday's dreams are tomorrow's promises. And tomorrow would be her wedding day. . . . What better promise could there be?

Silhouette Desire
15-Day Trial Offer

A new romance series
that explores
contemporary relationships
in exciting detail

Six Silhouette Desire romances, free for 15 days!
We'll send you six new Silhouette Desire romances
to look over for 15 days, absolutely free! If you decide
not to keep the books, return them and owe nothing.

Six books a month, free home delivery. If you like
Silhouette Desire romances as much as we think you
will, keep them and return your payment with the
invoice. Then we will send you six new books every
month to preview, just as soon as they are published.
You pay only for the books you decide to keep, and
you never pay postage and handling.

Silhouette Desire

Coming Next Month

Price of Surrender by Stephanie James

Holt Sinclair thought everything had its price until he met a woman who couldn't be bought. Adena West had come to him on business but Holt was more interested in pleasure. She entered his corporate jungle to become passion's prey.

Sweet Serenity by Billie Douglass

When Serena was a child, Tom Reynolds destroyed her happy life. With Tom's reappearance all the old hurt returned. Although he made her tremble with passion, Serena vowed not to fall beneath his spell.

Gentle Conquest by Kathryn Mallory

When rock star Stuart North agreed to buy and preserve historic Brogan House, he wanted gray-eyed Robin Elliot as part of the deal. What he didn't bargain for was the electricity between them that burst into a flashfire of passion.

Coming Next Month

Seduction by Design by Erin St. Claire

From the very beginning Tyler Scott made his intentions clear to Hailey — he intended to be her lover. He radiated a raw masculine power that left Hailey helpless with desire and unable to resist him.

Shadow of Betrayal by Nicole Monet

Diana Moreland tried to hate Joshua Cambridge especially now that he returned to claim his son; the nephew she raised all alone. Desperately she fought to keep the child and her heart — and lost both.

Ask Me No Secrets by Ruth Stewart

The past was behind her, and when Allison looked into Forrest Bennett's coal-black eyes she knew the future held a glowing promise of love. But would he love her still when he penetrated to the secret heart of her passion?

YOU'LL BE SWEPT AWAY
WITH SILHOUETTE DESIRE

$1.75 each

1 ☐ CORPORATE AFFAIR
James

2 ☐ LOVE'S SILVER WEB
Monet

3 ☐ WISE FOLLY
Clay

4 ☐ KISS AND TELL Carey

5 ☐ WHEN LAST WE LOVED
Baker

6 ☐ A FRENCHMAN'S KISS
Mallory

7 ☐ NOT EVEN FOR LOVE
Claire

8 ☐ MAKE NO PROMISES
Dee

9 ☐ MOMENT IN TIME
Simms

10 ☐ WHENEVER I LOVE YOU
Smith

$1.95 each

11 ☐ VELVET TOUCH
James

12 ☐ THE COWBOY AND THE
LADY Palmer

13 ☐ COME BACK, MY LOVE
Wallace

14 ☐ BLANKET OF STARS
Valley

15 ☐ SWEET BONDAGE
Vernon

16 ☐ DREAM COME TRUE
Major

17 ☐ OF PASSION BORN
Simms

18 ☐ SECOND HARVEST
Ross

19 ☐ LOVER IN PURSUIT
James

20 ☐ KING OF DIAMONDS
Allison

21 ☐ LOVE IN THE CHINA SEA
Baker

22 ☐ BITTERSWEET IN BERN
Durant

23 ☐ CONSTANT STRANGER
Sunshine

24 ☐ SHARED MOMENTS
Baxter

25 ☐ RENAISSANCE MAN
James

26 ☐ SEPTEMBER MORNING
Palmer

27 ☐ ON WINGS OF NIGHT
Conrad

28 ☐ PASSIONATE JOURNEY
Lovan

29 ☐ ENCHANTED DESERT
Michelle

30 ☐ PAST FORGETTING
Lind

31 ☐ RECKLESS PASSION
James

32 ☐ YESTERDAY'S DREAMS
Clay

33 ☐ PROMISE ME
TOMORROW Powers

34 ☐ SNOW SPIRIT
Milan

35 ☐ MEANT TO BE
Major

36 ☐ FIRES OF MEMORY
Summers

- -

SILHOUETTE DESIRE, Department SD/6
1230 Avenue of the Americas
New York, NY 10020

Please send me the books I have checked above. I am enclosing $_____
(please add 50¢ to cover postage and handling. NYS and NYC residents please add
appropriate sales tax.) Send check or money order—no cash or C.O.D.'s please.
Allow six weeks for delivery.

NAME _____

ADDRESS _____

CITY _____ STATE/ZIP _____